UNCLE MISHA'S PARTISANS

UNCLE MISHA'S PARTISANS

YURI SUHL

FOUR WINDS PRESS | NEW YORK

Also by Yuri Suhl:

Fiction:

ONE FOOT IN AMERICA
COWBOY ON A WOODEN HORSE

Biography:

ERNESTINE ROSE AND THE BATTLE FOR HUMAN RIGHTS
ELOQUENT CRUSADER: ERNESTINE ROSE

Documentary:

THEY FOUGHT BACK: THE STORY OF JEWISH RESISTANCE
IN NAZI EUROPE

Childrens Books:

SIMON BOOM GIVES A WEDDING
AN ALBUM OF THE JEWS IN AMERICA

Published by Four Winds Press.
A Division of Scholastic Magazines, Inc., New York, N.Y.
Copyright © 1973 by Yuri Suhl.
All rights reserved.
Printed in the United States of America.
Library of Congress Catalogue Card Number: 73-76459
1 2 3 4 5 77 76 75 74 73

*Though most of the characters,
places and events described
in this book are fictitious,
the story was inspired
by an actual episode.*

UNCLE MISHA'S PARTISANS

1 Dawn came suddenly with a burst of bright red that changed quickly to pink, to purple, to pale blue. But the two riders on horseback had not a moment to reflect on this spectacular play of color. They were Jewish partisans and only four hours earlier they had blown up a German troop train heading east. Now they were galloping at top speed to Klynov, the one Ukrainian village in the region where they'd be safe from pursuers. Klynov was six kilometers from the forest where Uncle Misha's partisans were based. The Germans dared not set foot in Klynov.

They knew that by this time every police station and troop garrison along their way had been alerted to be on the lookout for bandits—the Germans' name for partisans. Knowing the terrain of the region, they bypassed all the towns and villages where the danger was greatest and took out-of-the-way paths known only to the local population. Wherever possible they hugged the edge of a forest. The forest was the partisans' domain. Here every tree was an ally, a fortress.

The two had hardly exchanged a word since they had left behind them a heap of mangled steel, flying bodies, and fires lighting up the sky for miles around. Galloping single-file, they would have had to shout to make themselves heard. In the stillness of the night their own voices could betray them to the enemy. It was not until they came to a crossroads where a crude wooden sign in the shape of an arrow said "Klynov," that they reduced their horses' gallop to a brisk trot and pulled up alongside each other.

Berek, the younger of the two, spoke first: "That was quite a candle you lighted up there, Yoshke." He looked younger than his twenty-five years as he smiled at his comrade.

"One candle? I could swear I saw about six fires going before we took off."

"I'm referring to the one you set off with your grenade. That was no fire, Yoshke. That was Gehenna itself shooting up into the sky. I haven't heard such a roar or seen such a flame in all my life."

"I must admit it was quite a torch," Yoshke chuckled with satisfaction. "Here are all these cars one on top of the other and there this one stands all by itself like an orphan. So something had to be done. Right?"

"Right," Berek said, and leaned over as far as he could to slap Yoshke on the back.

Berek was known to his fellow partisans as "the engineer" although he had never seen the inside of an engineering school. He was a marvel with things mechanical. He could take a rusty old gun, considered worthless by everyone, and make it "sing" again. He could defuse a land mine, manufacture a time bomb, create a deadly explosive device from an empty sardine can and a few scraps of dynamite. He could repair anything from a wristwatch to a motorcycle. And all this in a forest, without any tools to speak of. To a partisan detachment Berek was worth his weight in gold.

For Yoshke, it was a happy moment. To have been picked by this genius of the pliers and screwdriver as his partner for this important mission was honor enough. And now to be complimented by him with this gesture more eloquent than words!

The sun had risen to its full roundness now and blended all the colors of daybreak into one fiery red. But the two partisans were still preoccupied with the flame of their own creation when the distant drone of a propeller broke into their thoughts. They brought their horses to a halt and gazed up at the sky. The black dot they saw moving swiftly in their direction was still too high up for recognition.

"Could be one of our own," Yoshke said, hopefully.

"Could also be a Stuka. The dogs may have caught up with us."

They dismounted quickly and made for the nearby field where they flopped down on a bed of tall grass, still wet from the dew. In a matter of minutes the faint buzz had turned into a deafening roar and the field was sprayed with bullets all around them. Repeatedly the plane dived low, circled, and sprayed while the two lay motionless, holding their breaths. They lay frozen in their positions long after the plane had moved on. When they could no longer hear the faintest sound of a propeller they rose to their feet.

Miraculously the horses had not been hit. They were huddled by a tree a short distance off the road. "See, even the horses know something about camouflage," Berek said as they were walking back.

"They're creatures of habit," said Yoshke, a former coachman who knew much about horses. "In the forest we keep them tied to trees, so they walked to the nearest tree." As if to illustrate his point Yoshke called them with his familiar whistle and they responded.

They were almost at the edge of the field about to step off onto the road when Berek grabbed Yoshke's arm. "Look at this," he said, pointing to a body sprawled on the ground, face down, the right hand clutching a violin case. The clothing too was odd. An ordinary peasant's cap and a military coat of the Russian variety long enough to cover the boots down to the heels. Coming upon bodies in fields was not unusual in wartime. But this one was baffling.

Yoshke bent down and turned the body over. To their surprise it was not a man they had come upon but a boy. And he stared at them not with the glazed eyes of a corpse but with the eyes of a frightened youth, pleading not to be hurt.

Yoshke took the boy's free hand and helped him up. His oversized soldier's overcoat, with only one brass button left in the middle, touched the ground, completely hiding his feet. The long sleeves hid his hands so that the violin case which he pressed to himself seemed to be held with a handless hand. His cap, a size or two too large for his head, kept falling over his eyes, and his small neck swam in the enormous ring of his coat collar. All together the youth had a comical look, inviting laughter. But when one glimpsed the deep sadness in his black eyes, a sadness that spread over his pale face, the impulse to laugh gave way to a surge of sympathy and concern.

"Where are you from?" Berek asked.

"Stare-Mloda," the boy replied in a barely audible voice.

Berek turned to Yoshke.

"I've heard of it," Yoshke said. "A long way from here."

"Sixty kilometers," the boy volunteered.

"What are you doing here, so far away from home?"

"I don't have a home," the boy said. "The Nazis killed my parents and my sister."

"What's your name?" Yoshke asked.

"Mitek," the boy said.

The two partisans exchanged a look. Mitek was a

Ukrainian name and the boy spoke Ukrainian fluently.

"Why did the Nazis kill your parents? What had they done?"

"My parents?"

"Yes. What had they done?"

"Nothing. They were Jews." He had not mentioned this to anyone in a year. In his wanderings from village to village he was Mitek, a Ukrainian orphan of whom there were many. When pressed for details, he always gave the same believable story. The Germans put fire to all the huts in his village. His parents and sister were at home when it happened. He alone was out in the field at the time. He wasn't sure these two were Jews. But they were partisans. That he could see. So it was safe to tell the truth. What a relief not to have to lie!

"And how did you manage to save your life?" Berek asked.

"I was in town for my violin lesson that day. When I came home I found everyone dead and all the things gone. Furniture and everything. A neighbor took me in and let me sleep in his barn for a few nights. Then he told me I would have to leave because everyone in the village knew who I was. He told me to go to a village where no one knew me and not to tell anyone I was Jewish. It was summer and I could get work helping in the field, or as a shepherd. When there was no work, I played the violin at parties or weddings. I also sing a little," he added self-consciously.

"What kind of songs do you sing?" Berek wanted to know.

"Ukranian. Russian. . . ."

"Know any Yiddish songs?" Yoshke asked.

The boy thought hard, twisting the only button on his coat. "Yiddish I know two," he finally said. " *'Oifn Pripetchik'* and *'Lomir Sich Iberbeten.'* My Jewish name is Motele," he added, as if to make up for his limited Yiddish repertoire.

"And where are you headed for now?" said Berek.

"A village called Klynov, about six kilometers from here."

"Got a job there?"

The boy shook his head. "I'm not going there to work. I'm going there to look for Uncle Misha's partisans."

"How do you know about Uncle Misha's partisans?"

"From the police."

"The police no less!" Yoshke exclaimed.

"I suppose you just walked into the police station," Berek continued, "and you said, 'Pardon me, sir. I am looking for Uncle Misha's partisans. Can you help me find them?' And the police captain said, 'Certainly, we'll be happy to help you. You have to get to a village called Klynov, about six kilometers from the crossroads, and there you'll find Uncle Misha's partisans.' Isn't that the way it happened?"

"No. That's not the way it happened," the boy said, smiling for the first time since they had found him.

"All right, then you tell us."

"I was working for a peasant in a village called Pielec," the boy began. "The peasant's daughter married a policeman. After the church wedding there was a big party in the peasant's house. There were many policemen there. . . ."

"About how many would you say?" Berek wanted to know.

"About ten, twelve maybe. They came from other villages too. I had to play for them and they danced with the village girls. They drank a lot of vodka and some of them got very drunk. They talked about Jews. How many this one caught and how many that one caught. . . ."

"Caught where, in ghettos?"

"In villages where they were hiding. They talked about the partisans and one of them said there were hundreds of Jewish partisans in the Zhitomir forest near Klynov, and that the commander's name was Uncle Misha and that he was also a Jew. The next day, when it got light, I sneaked out of the barn where I slept, and escaped."

"And what will you do when you get to Uncle Misha's partisans," Yoshke asked, "play the fiddle?"

"I'll do what they tell me to. I can ride a horse," he added after a pause.

"I think the best place for him would be the family camp," Berek said to Yoshke, "don't you think?"

Yoshke nodded. "What will a kid like him do in a combat detachment?"

"How old are you?" Berek asked.

"Twelve," the boy replied, raising himself slightly on his toes.

"In the family camp they'll find something for him to do," Yoshke said, "and he'll have boys his age to play with."

"I'm not looking for boys to play with," the boy said. "I want to be a partisan."

A loud neighing came from the road. Now it was the horses calling them. "The animals must be very thirsty," Yoshke said. "Come on, young man," he took the boy's arm and led him as they waded through the tall grass. "You say you can ride a horse?"

"Yes."

"Well, this time you'll share one. With me. You'll ride in the back and hold on to me. But what will we do with your fiddle? You can't hold on to me and the fiddle at the same time."

"I'll hold the violin with one hand and hold on to you with the other."

"That won't do," Yoshke shook his head. "My horse sometimes forgets he's a horse and thinks he's an eagle. Berek," he turned to his partner, "I'm taking the boy. Will you take the fiddle?"

"And what will I hold the reins with, my teeth?"

Yoshke tried holding the violin case with his left hand the reins with the right one but it didn't work. The case had no handle and he had to press it to his chest. It was a clumsy, hazardous arrangement. In the end it was the boy himself who solved the problem. The partisans carried their automatic rifles strapped to their backs, and that gave him an idea. He untied the rope from his coat and handed it to Yoshke. "Here," he said, "tie the fiddle to my back so all our hands will be free."

"The boy has a head on his shoulders," Yoshke said as he fastened the case to Motele's back. Then he helped him up on the horse before he got on it himself.

The sun was up high now and the sky was a clear blue. It was a September morning, bright and cool. The grass, the foliage, were still green. Every now and then a strong breeze would swirl through the air and when that happened the tall grass bowed low and the trees applauded with their leaves. Then, as suddenly as it came up, the breeze died down and nothing moved except the two horses clopping along at a leisurely trot. The two partisans, pleasantly fatigued by the long and eventful night, yielded to the horses' own pace and relaxed.

They rode on in silence, each with his thoughts, and Motele remembered that this was how he had ridden with his father to the flour mill on certain days of the week; his father sitting up front on their white, yellow-spotted horse Hushko, and he in the back, his arms around his father. The memory saddened him. He loved his father dearly and whenever he thought about him he recalled that afternoon when he found him dead on the bare floor next to his mother and sister. Right now if he were alone he might have cried, as he frequently did in some peasant's barn at night. But he was with partisans. He brushed his eyes quickly with his sleeve and called out to Yoshke, "Do you have children?"

After a long pause Yoshke replied, "I *had* children."

Motele said no more. He put his arms tightly around Yoshke as he used to when he rode with his father.

2 "That's Klynov," Yoshke said to the boy as they entered the village. To their left, and clearly visible, was the vast expanse of the dense Zhitomir forest. To their right in about a dozen scattered huts people were stirring themselves to life for the new day. Ahead of them was a long straight road, part paved, part dirt, that led to Ovrutch, the county seat and a German stronghold. Midway between Klynov and Ovrutch stood an old wooden bridge, spanning a narrow river. It was heavily guarded. Anyone approaching the bridge from the direction of Klynov was suspected of being a partisan, or a spy for Uncle Misha's detachment.

When they turned left they were on the last stretch of their journey, a narrow path that took them straight to the forest. Motele kept turning his head excitedly from one side of Yoshke's broad back to the other. He had wandered for days in search of this forest and now he was here. Soon he would see what a partisan detachment looked like, and maybe he would see the commander. Uncle Misha himself. Just thinking about it made his heart beat faster.

But what about that family camp Berek had mentioned back there in the field? He didn't know what a family camp was, but if it wasn't a place for real partisans who go out to fight the Nazis then he knew he wouldn't like it. There must be something a boy his age could do to make himself useful to real partisans. He could ride a horse. He could feed the animals, if they had any. He could play and sing for them. He would tell all this to Uncle Misha and beg him not to send him to a family camp. Still he was curious. He was about to tap Yoshke on the back and say, "What's a family camp?" But he changed his mind. Maybe he'd forgotten about it, so why remind him?

Suddenly he was startled by a voice that seemed to have come from nowhere, *"Gut morgen,"* the voice called out in Yiddish.

"Gut morgen," Yoshke and Berek replied, glancing up. They rode on without saying a word, as though it were natural to be greeted in Yiddish by trees. This time Motele did tap Yoshke on the back. "Who was that?" he asked.

"A partisan on guard duty."

"I didn't see him."

"Neither did I. You're not supposed to be able to see him. He's supposed to see you."

"Is he very high up?"

"There's a ledge attached to the middle of the tree. That's where he sits with the automatic in his hand. Both he and the gun are so well camouflaged that you can't tell them apart from the tree."

"Is he on the lookout for Germans?"

"Not just Germans," Yoshke said. "Anybody wandering into this forest better know the password or he'll be shot."

"Is *gut morgen* the password?"

Both men chuckled with amusement, "No," Yoshke said, "*gut morgen* is not a password."

"And neither is *gut ovent*," Berek said, still chuckling.

"You see, Motele," Yoshke explained, "in daytime the guard can see who we are, so there's no need to ask for the password."

Motele felt embarrassed. Why didn't he think of it himself? Why did he have to ask a foolish question? Now they'll think he isn't smart enough to be a partisan and they'll surely send him to that family camp. "I can climb trees very fast," he announced, loud enough for both to hear him.

"Would you want to be a guard?" Yoshke asked.

"Yes," he said, eagerly.

"Maybe you'll become one. The family camp also has guards."

Motele didn't open his mouth again until they reached the partisan base.

As they approached the base several partisans came running toward them, waving and shouting greetings. And when they heard that the mission was successful they let out a shout of joy that brought others to the scene, including Uncle Misha. Yoshke and Berek dismounted, and Motele, eager to impress Uncle Misha, didn't wait for Yoshke to give him a hand. But he hadn't reckoned with the violin case. He fell and had to be helped to his feet by one of the partisans. Luckily he wasn't hurt. But it was embarrassing. And why did he have to blush in front of everybody? Right now he wished he could vanish; disappear from sight, and perhaps try again with better luck.

Yoshke put his arm around the boy. "This is Motele," he said. "He was on his way to Klynov to look for Uncle Misha's partisans. So we gave him a ride and saved him the trouble. He plays the fiddle and can sing all kinds of songs. And now he wants to become a partisan. Am I right, Motele?"

Motele nodded, pleased with what Yoshke said, and when Uncle Misha extended his hand Motele gave the commander a vigorous handshake, as befitted a would-be partisan. He wondered why he was called Uncle Misha when he didn't look at all as old as an uncle was supposed to look. And he didn't look at all like a commander of partisans. He was a bald-headed man with eyeglasses who reminded him of his music teacher. And the jacket he wore was that of an ordinary soldier. But he did have a medal attached to it, a red star.

"What ghetto did you escape from, Motele?" Uncle Misha asked.

"I was not in a ghetto."

"Lucky fellow," one of the partisans said.

Motele fell silent. A look of sadness darkened his pale face. How could he feel lucky when his parents and sister were dead?

"The boy is an orphan," Yoshke explained. "The Hitlerites killed his parents before they even got to a ghetto."

"My sister too." Motele added, looking straight at Uncle Misha so that he would know why he was here. How he loved his sister, Basha. He used to tell her everything, even his secrets. She was only one year older than he, but she was so wise. It was like having a third parent who was your age and was also a friend with whom you could play when you felt like it and be serious too. And she had such a lovely voice. Sometimes they would sit by the lake, or walk through the field and sing together for hours.

And he still talked to her even though he knew she was dead. That night after the wedding party, when he was alone in the barn remembering what the policemen had said about Uncle Misha and the Jewish partisans, he had confided in Basha his secret to leave. "Tomorrow I'm going far away from here, Basha. Far away to the Zhitomir forest where Uncle Misha and his partisans are hiding out. You know what partisans do? They fight the Germans. They take revenge for what the Germans did. The villages they burned. The peasants they killed. I'll tell them what they did to you and to Papa and to Mama. They'll make the Germans pay for it, you'll see. And I'll do it too. Because I'll be a partisan. Am I afraid? No. Partisans are not afraid of anything."

He knew she couldn't talk anymore. But that night, in the barn, he could hear her voice as clearly as though she were alive. And he could hear it now, just as clear as in the barn. "Tell them, tell them," her voice rang out. "You said you'd tell them. Why don't you?"

He was startled and looked about him to see if the others had heard it too. They must have. Or why would they all stare at him so? "Go on, tell him," the voice urged him on.

"But Yoshke has already told them," he wanted to say. But he didn't. It was one thing to talk to his dead sister when he was alone in the field, or in the barn. But here, with the partisans staring at him, he couldn't.

"No, *you* tell them," he heard Basha say. "Are you afraid? You said partisans are not afraid of anything."

He straightened up to appear as tall as he possibly could and, speaking directly to Uncle Misha, said, "I came home from my violin lesson and found them all dead. My father, my mother, and Basha—my sister. They were all on the floor. The next day they hanged the school teacher from a tree."

"Was he a Jew?" Uncle Misha asked.

"No. He was a Ukrainian."

"What else did the Hitlerites do in your village?"

"They set fire to some huts with the people in them."

"Was yours the only Jewish family in the village?"

"Yes. There were some Jewish families in Pieska. That's the next village from ours."

"And what happened to them?"

"They were all shot by the Germans."

"That's how it was in the villages," he heard Uncle Misha say to the others. "They didn't even bother to take them to a ghetto. They shot them on the spot." He turned to Yoshke and Berek. "Have a bite of food. Rest up. And then you'll come to my tent and give me a full report."

"Uncle Misha."

"Yes, Motele?"

"Can I be a partisan? I can ride a horse . . . and . . . ." Oh, if he could only think of something else he could do besides playing the violin and singing songs . . . "And I'm not afraid . . . ." He'd said it! He'd said everything Basha wanted him to say. And his face didn't grow red. And he didn't twist the button on his coat. And now he looked straight at Uncle Misha, waiting for his decision.

"Of course you can be a partisan. And you'll be a brave partisan, I'm sure. We'll talk more about that later, when you have had something to eat and have rested."

What should he do now, he wondered. Salute? Say,

Thank you, Uncle Misha? He didn't know. And before he could make up his mind what to do they were already walking toward the base, Berek leading his horse by the reins and Yoshke his.

"Let me," he cried out, taking the reins from Yoshke. With one hand he held on to the violin case and with the other he clutched the reins. He was leading a partisan's horse and it followed him willingly. Oh, if only Basha could see him now!

3 It was still very early in the morning but the partisans were up and the base was bustling with activity. Some already had their breakfast and were getting ready to go out on their assigned missions. Others, men who had just returned from long journeys, or those who were recovering from wounds and were not yet fit for combat, were all busy with their tasks around the base—tending to the horses, storing away provisions, cleaning their guns. Berek already knew what he would be doing as soon as he had a few hours of sleep—fixing everything that needed fixing. And Yoshke? There was no telling what he would be doing. Most likely he would go out on a food expedition. There were several hundred partisans in the detachment that had to be fed. This made it necessary to continuously comb the villages for food. Some peasants gave willingly, others had to be coerced. Yoshke was frequently on such a detail.

"Let's see if we can find you a mess kit," Yoshke said. "You can't drink hot chicory from your bare hands."

Motele followed Yoshke to the supply tent, a structure that resembled a tent only in shape. Instead of canvas its sloping walls consisted of twigs and branches covered with slabs of earth to catch the rain. Yoshke had to lower his head as he entered.

After the bright daylight outside, it took Motele a moment or two to adjust to the dimness of the tent, but soon things became visible. A heap of blankets, a heap of German uniforms, a heap of civilian clothes all neatly folded and stacked. Guns lying across two wooden horses, a pail of grenades, and parts of guns. In the center of this motley assortment sat the partisan in charge of supplies, on a wooden keg, eating his breakfast.

"Good morning, Avremel," Yoshke boomed out a hearty greeting and extended his hand.

Avremel, a short bald-headed man wearing a military jacket that resembled Uncle Misha's, rose, put his mess kit down on the keg, and, taking Yoshke's hand in both of his, shook it vigorously. "Good morning, good morning, Yoshke. And congratulations. I already heard the good news." He sized up Motele. "And I see you brought yourself a musician to celebrate."

"This is Motele, our new partisan," Yoshke said, putting his arm around the boy.

Avremel pointed to the violin case. "What do you keep in there?" he said, "a regular fiddle or your underwear?"

Motele smiled. The thought of underwear in a violin case struck him as very odd, even funny. "A regular fiddle," he said, using Avremel's words. "You want to see?" He was about to snap the case open but Avremel held up his hand. "I believe you. I believe you. I take your word for it." In a more serious tone he added, "And where is the boy from? What ghetto?"

"Avremel," Yoshke pleaded, "do me a favor and save these questions for later. He's not running away from here. Right now find him a mess kit so he can put something warm into himself. And I could also use something warm."

"A mess kit for the boy." Avremel became thoughtful and held his index finger to his forehead, as though he were pressing a memory button. Then he turned abruptly, made his way through all the heaps to the back of the tent and rummaged through a heap of bric-a-brac. "I have it," he announced triumphantly, holding his find aloft. As he handed Motele the kit he said, "You can leave the fiddle here if you want. Why drag it to the kitchen?"

Motele looked up at Yoshke.

"Good idea," Yoshke said. "It'll free your hands." He saw the hesitation in Motele's face. "It's all right, it's safe," he assured him.

Reluctantly Motele handed Avremel the case and watched him place it carefully on a heap of blankets. The violin was his most precious possession. It was more than a musical instrument now; it had become a means of staying alive. When there was no work for him as a shepherd or a field hand it was the violin that saved him from the indignities of an ordinary beggar. Instead of holding out his hand he would strike up a tune and give the peasants something in return for their slab of bread, or bowl of soup. And sometimes, when he was very tired and the ache of loneliness made it difficult to go on, he would wander off to some field where he was all alone and take out his violin and play. He would play everything he remembered, the sad as well as the happier pieces, and the playing would take him back to the time when he had a home, and parents, and a sister. And it would seem to him that Basha was sitting near him, as she always did when he practiced, her hands on her knees, her head low, her eyes closed, lost completely in the sounds he brought forth. And when he'd finished she would open her eyes, let out a sigh, as though she had held her breath throughout the time he was playing, look into his face and say, "You play beautifully, Motele."

What Yoshke called the kitchen turned out to be an outdoor fire over which hung a huge copper kettle suspended from an iron bar. Except for parts around the rim, the kettle was blackened by the flames that leaped up to lick it. A tall, powerful-looking man in a woolen shirt with rolled up sleeves ladled out the chicory, a dark steaming liquid, into the open mess kits the partisans held out to him. From there they went to the near-

by table—two rough boards on a pair of wooden horses
—where another man placed a slab of black bread and
a chunk of hard salami on the other half of the divided
metal dish. With the breakfast in his hands the partisan
picked the nearest tree and squatted down to eat.

As soon as the partisans discovered that there was a
young boy in their midst the orderly moving line suddenly slowed down and was twisted out of shape. Feet
shuffled forward on their own while bodies leaned out
sideways and heads turned to catch a glimpse of the
new arrival. Even the man with the ladle in his hand
peered over the heads of the others to where the boy
stood.

Why are they all staring at me so? Motele wondered.
Haven't they seen a boy before? Maybe it's because
they're all grown men and I'm the only boy, he told
himself. He looked up at Yoshke, silently asking for an
explanation, but Yoshke merely smiled at him and
nodded. After a while the many eyes on him made him
uncomfortable. He lowered his head.

Some partisans couldn't control their urge to touch
Motele. To talk to him. They gave up their place in
line and ran up to him. They shook hands with him.
"What's your name?"

"Motele."

"Motele," they would repeat nodding thoughtfully.
"From what ghetto?"

Here is where Yoshke came to his aid. "The boy was not in a ghetto."

"On the Aryan side."

"In a village. His father was a miller."

"The boy is an orphan?"

Yoshke nodded. "They shot his parents."

"My sister too," Motele added.

"Motele," they would repeat the name slowly, as though they were caressing it, and their faces grew very sad.

Were they pitying him because he was an orphan? Suddenly he remembered what Yoshke had told him earlier, on the way to Klynov, "I *had* children," and he understood their sadness.

He had never had chicory for breakfast. At home his mother used to give him and Basha warm milk and buttered white rolls which she herself had baked. The chicory she and his father drank was whitened with milk and sweetened with sugar. But this chicory was black and bitter. He would have been happier without it, but if partisans drank black and bitter chicory so would he.

Yoshke seemed to enjoy every bit of it, announcing his pleasure with grunts of satisfaction after each sip. Motele wondered whether he would ever get to like chicory that much. He watched Yoshke eat and imitated him. First he broke off a chunk of bread and pushed it into his mouth. Then he cut off a piece of salami with his penknife and used the tip of the knife for a fork. Then he washed it all down with a swallow of chicory. But Yoshke finished ahead of him and, after wiping his mouth with the back of his hand, said, "Feels good to put something warm inside you, doesn't it Motele?"

Motele hesitated a moment and decided to say yes. What kind of a partisan would Yoshke think he'd make if he'd said no to chicory? Besides, he was going to drink that bitter stuff from now on, and get used to it and maybe even learn to like it enough to grunt like Yoshke.

When he had drained off the last drop his eye caught something that gave him a start. Stamped into the bottom of the mess kit was the trademark of Hitler's Third Reich—a swastika! The sign that had come to mean only one thing to him—death. The death of his parents and sister. The death of his school teacher hanging from a tree. The death of peasants roasted alive in their burning huts. How could Jewish partisans eat from such dishes? The thought that he had just taken food from this one was enough to make him want to throw up. "Yoshke, look!" he pushed the kit in front of him.

"You drank it all up. Good boy."

"I mean this," he pointed to the swastika.

"This? I think I have one too." He picked up the empty kit from the ground and showed it to Motele. The same swastika. "We took them off some dead Fritzes," Yoshke explained. "When a partisan has one of these it means one Hitlerite less in this world. We always take their weapons first. And when there's time we take other things—their mess kits, their boots, even their uniforms."

Now he knew where the German uniforms he saw in Avremel's tent came from—dead Fritzes.

"Are all the mess kits here German?" Motele asked.

"We've all kinds. Most of them are Russian. When Hitler attacked and the Russians had to retreat in a hurry they left behind them lots of supplies. The peasants got a hold of some of them and hid them and later sold them. And some of them got into the hands of partisans. Uncle Misha wears a Russian military jacket."

"Avremel too."

"That's right. You have a good eye."

"This is Russian too," Motele said, pointing to his coat.

"Yes, but you sweep the ground with it. We'll have to talk to Avremel and see if he can dig up something that'll fit you better."

And maybe he could find a Russian mess kit for me, Motele thought. Despite what Yoshke said he would still prefer to eat from a dish that didn't have a swastika stamped on it. He pointed to Yoshke's automatic and said, "Did you take it off a dead Fritz?"

"That's a Russian Vyntovka," Yoshke patted the weapon. "Seventy rounds to a clip. Every partisan dreams of owning a Vyntovka."

"Where did you get the Vyntovka?"

"Where did I get the Vyntovka?" Yoshke scratched his thick brush of a beard that covered much of his big face. "That's a story for some other time. Not when we're sleepy."

"I'm not sleepy."

"But I am."

"Tell me," the boy pleaded, his eyes ablaze with curiosity.

Yoshke put his large hand on the boy's head and shook it good-naturedly back and forth. "What am I to do with you? All right." Then he raised himself a little against the tree to get more support for his back, and began the story: "That goes back to the time when we weren't yet a detachment, when we were just nineteen Jews who had escaped from the Koretz ghetto together with Uncle Misha. And the only weapon we had between us then was one Russian pistol, which Uncle Misha had managed to buy from a peasant for a large sum of money. One pistol for nineteen Jews who wanted to become partisans. . . ."

"So what happened?" Motele moved up closer to Yoshke not to miss a single expression of his face.

"Money we didn't have. Food we didn't have. Weapons we didn't have. During the day we had to hide in the forest and at night we didn't know on what door to knock. Believe me we were not to be envied. One evening, as we were sitting on the ground, each with his own sad thoughts, Uncle Misha said to us, 'Jews, don't despair. We've come this far, we'll stay. Going back to the ghetto means going back to a certain death. This one revolver will help us get another and the rest we'll get with our bare hands. Tomorrow, before the sun rises, three of us will slip out of the forest and hide in the thickets by the road. The first Hitlerite that comes along we'll waylay and take his weapon. We'll lie in wait for him even if it takes all day.' " 'I'm one of the three, Misha,' I called out."

"Was Berek the other?"

"Berek wasn't even with us then. He came later, from a different ghetto. But there were plenty of volunteers. Almost everyone wanted to go. In the end Misha picked a young man named Shimshen. We called him the Red Shimshen because of his red hair. Unfortunately Shimshen is no longer with us. He was our first casualty a few weeks later. He was a very brave fellow."

"So what happened that morning?"

"What happened that morning was that we got three Hitlerites instead of one. That was around nine in the morning and we had been lying there since four. Suddenly we see three Ukrainian policemen leading six Ukrainian youths, boys no more than sixteen or seventeen. . . ."

"You said Hitlerites."

"And what is a Ukrainian policeman, not a Hitlerite? Even worse. By working for the Germans he betrays his own people."

"So what happened?"

"Don't interrupt so you'll hear what happened. One

policeman walked in front of the boys and the other two behind them. They were three and we were three, only they had a rifle each and we had one pistol among us. What should we do? We had less than a minute to decide. We decided we must take the chance. But to shoot from the thicket was too risky because we might hit one of the boys. So Uncle Misha, who had the pistol, gave a shot in the air and we all rushed out, shouting "Hurrah!" so loud they must have thought there were twenty of us. The unexpected shot and hurrah confused them and before they managed to come to their senses Uncle Misha shot one of them, I had my arm around the throat of another, and Shimshen was already grappling with the third on the ground. In the midst of all this the six boys took to their heels and vanished. A few minutes later we vanished and we took with us three German rifles and left behind us three Ukrainian fascists, dead on the road." Yoshke was rubbing his eyes. He had difficulty keeping them open. "The rest I'll tell you later," he said. "Right now let's go to my tent for a nap."

"Tell me just a little bit more," Motele begged.

Yoshke looked at the boy's face, so alive with eagerness. It had been a long time since a boy his age had asked him for something. "All right," he agreed, "just a little more and then we go to sleep. Where was I?"

"You had three German rifles," Motele reminded him.

"Yes. We returned to the forest with a whole arsenal.

You can imagine the rejoicing. We were very hungry but we knew that that night we would eat. We knew that as soon as it got dark we would go to the village. When you have three rifles you can knock on any door and get food. Well, it turned out we didn't have to go to the village that night. Instead of us going for food, the food came to us. As soon as it got dark two of the six boys we saw that morning came to us, bringing a basket of food. They said they came to thank us for freeing them from the police. 'Where were they taking you?' Uncle Misha asked. 'To the *Arbeitsamt* in Ovrutch,' one of them said. 'From there the Germans were to send us to Germany for slave labor. They said we'd be working on farms, but we heard from other boys who were taken that we'd end up working in munition factories or in the Bavarian coal mines.' "

"What was in the basket?"

"A feast. Hardboiled eggs, roasted potatoes, bread and butter, milk, apples, pears, cherries, things we hadn't seen the whole year in the ghetto. And they told us about the village, whom we could trust and whom we couldn't. And they warned us against the forester who worked for the Germans. He had discovered three unarmed Jews in the forest and handed them over to the Gestapo. Later he boasted in the village that his reward was two quarts of vodka for each Jew. That same forester is also responsible for the death of two Russian partisans whose detachment had to move to another base while they were away on a mission. He found them wandering in the forest and promised to lead them to their detachment. Instead he led them straight into the hands of the Germans, who hanged them in the center of the village. He later boasted that for the partisans his reward was, in addition to the vodka, two kilos of sugar. Well, that night we took turns standing guard while the others slept. And talking about sleeping, I can't keep my eyes open. Come, let's go."

"You haven't told me how you got your Vyntovka."

"Later, later. You're not running away and neither am I." He rose and took the boy by the hand. "I think you'll just about squeeze into my tent," Yoshke said, measuring him with his eyes.

"What about my violin?"

"Your fiddle is in good hands with Avremel. There's no room for the three of us."

Yoshke's tent was also made of twigs and branches, but it was so low and narrow Motele couldn't see how they'd both get in. Yoshke took off the automatic before he entered, then he bent down very low and slid onto the floor, which was covered with straw and served as a bed. He laid the automatic at his feet but didn't bother to take off the belt with the hand grenades. Then Motele slid in and together they filled up the tent. Yoshke pulled the thick horse blanket over both of them and said, "We'll sleep until they call us to lunch." Motele wondered how they would be called to lunch. He was about to ask but Yoshke was already asleep. He lay there, fixed in his position, afraid to stir lest he wake him, watching his large chest rise and fall to the rhythm of his breathing.

He had so much to tell Basha. He remembered when they used to trade stories. She would tell him everything she heard from her girl friends. And he would tell her what stories he heard from *his* friends, or from the people in the mill on days when his father took him along. And sometimes they would make one up themselves, each adding something to the story as they went along until they were pleased with the ending. But none of the stories they'd heard or made up was as exciting as the story Yoshke had told him this morning. And he hadn't even finished yet.

"Basha . . . ." He had whispered it so low the sound had barely touched his lips. "We must speak very quietly, Basha, so as not to wake Yoshke. Know what I had for breakfast?

"Chicory. It was black and tasted bitter. You wouldn't have liked it at all. I'll have to drink some more tomorrow I guess because that's what partisans have for breakfast. Bread, salami, and chicory." He was about to tell her about the swastika on the mess kit but changed his mind. It was a swastika man who had killed her, so why remind her of it. Sometimes when he talked to her he had a feeling that only he knew that Basha was dead but that Basha herself didn't know it. And he tried to remember not to tell her.

As he was about to begin the story his eyes closed and his lips wouldn't move even for a low whisper. He heard himself breathing in unison with Yoshke and fell asleep feeling pleasantly warm under the heavy blanket.

4 The ringing of a bell was pulling Motele out of a deep sleep. It sounded like the village church bell he heard on Sunday mornings. That meant he could stay in bed a little longer. There was no school on Sunday. His eyes still closed, he tried to hold on to a dream he'd been dreaming. Something about Basha and her girl friend chasing him through a field and catching him, and they all flopped down exhausted on the grass and couldn't stop giggling. There was more to the dream he wanted to remember, but the ringing had shattered it to bits that were rapidly dissolving into nothingness, like puffs of cloud torn by the wind. Then he opened his eyes, looked about him in the semidarkness of the tent, and remembered where he was.

Just when the bell had rung its last ring Yoshke opened his eyes, and sat bolt upright, his head nearly touching the roof of the tent. He grunted, yawned, and shook his head, as though shaking himself fully awake. "Are you up, Motele?"

"Yes."

"They're calling us to lunch." He pulled the blanket off both of them. "Come, let's put something warm inside us."

Motele hoped it wouldn't be chicory again. The mess kit! He hadn't changed it. What if Avremel didn't have another one? He thought of a way out. Whatever that something warm was he wouldn't finish it to the last drop. He'd leave a little bit on the bottom. Enough to cover the swastika.

The something warm turned out to be cabbage and potato soup with a few lima beans floating up whenever he put the spoon in. The bread was the same as they had had for breakfast, black and hard, easier to break with your fingers than with your teeth. Yoshke ate noisily and with relish. "Shmerke makes a good soup," he said, "even though it's always the same. Once in a great while he'll surprise you and make borsht. But that too will have some cabbage and potatoes in it."

"I never saw a man cook."

"If it were up to Shmerke, you think he'd be a cook? He's an ox of a man. Used to be a butcher before the war. He's still an ox except for his left foot. He was badly wounded on a mission. That was in the early days. Before we had a doctor. . . ."

"There's a doctor here?"

"Not here. In the family camp. At that time there was no family camp either. So poor Shmerke was laid up for months. The wound healed but it left him with a limp.

So he became our cook. I'll say this for him, he makes good cabbage and potato soup. Don't you like it?"

Motele nodded.

"Then why don't you finish it?"

"I'm full. He gave me too much."

"Then I'll finish it," Yoshke said, taking the canteen from him. "It's a sin to throw out food."

That's what his father used to say whenever he'd left some soup in his plate, even if it was only a spoonful. There were so many things about Yoshke that reminded him of his father. The way they rode the horse together. The way he tucked him in with the blanket. The way he was now finishing his leftover soup. He watched him put the dish to his mouth and drain the last drop from it. He was glad he didn't have to see that swastika again. "Will you finish the story now?"

"That's the end of the story. He was left with a limp so he became a cook."

"I mean how you got the Vyntovka."

"That story, Motele, is not for now. Right now I must get hold of Berek and go to Uncle Misha's tent to give him a full report of our mission. That can't wait. He must write it up and send it off to Partisan High Command in Moscow. I hear that Marshal Klementi Voroshilov himself reads Uncle Misha's reports. You know who Voroshilov is, don't you?"

Motele shook his head.

"He's Chief of the Partisan High Command." He

handed Motele his mess kit and added his own. "Rinse them both," he said, "and leave them in the tent."

"When will you be back?" Motele asked.

"In an hour. Maybe a little later. In the meantime you can have a look around the base. But don't go too far or you're bound to get lost. Forests are tricky that way. One tree leads to another and before you know it you're a long way from where you started."

Did Yoshke have to tell him that? He was a country boy, born and raised in a village. "I won't get lost. We lived near a forest."

"These are different times, Motele."

Times have changed but not forests. Then he remembered the warning about the forester. "I'll be careful," he promised.

"After that go to Avremel's tent. He will find something for you to do. And maybe he can dig up another coat for you. Even if it isn't your size. Something with buttons, so you won't have to hold it together with a rope. Tell him Yoshke said so." He put his big hand on Motele's head and rocked it back and forth. "I'll find you in Avremel's tent."

Not far from the "kitchen" stood two pails of water for the partisans to rinse their mess kits after each meal. He had watched Yoshke do it in the morning. First he gave the dish a rinse in one pail and then in the other, draining every drop off into the pail. "Water is precious in the forest," Yoshke had explained. "We have to haul it from Klynov in barrels. For cooking, for washing, and for the horses. Others let their horses graze in the fields and find their water at some stream. Our world is the forest and the horses must be with us all the time."

He'd mixed up the two mess kits in the rinsing and when he got to the tent he couldn't tell which was which. But what did it matter—they were both the same anyway. He put one down on the straw, next to Yoshke's Vyntovka and the other he pushed into his coat pocket to take with him to Avremel's tent. If he found a Russian one while helping Avremel he would exchange it without saying anything.

As he turned to go he hesitated, held back by an uneasy feeling that he wasn't doing the right thing. He was going to make it easier for himself, but what about Yoshke? If the sight of the swastika upset *him*, wasn't the same true of Yoshke? "I *had* children," he remembered Yoshke's words and the long silence that followed. He would change Yoshke's too. But as he reached down for the mess kit he hesitated again. What right had he to change Yoshke's dish without his permission? His own, that's something else. He let the dish lie and straightened up.

He started walking away and stopped. "No," he said to himself, resolutely, "either I change both or none." He pulled the mess kit from his pocket and tossed it down next to Yoshke's. He decided to talk to Yoshke about it. The way he felt about Yoshke he could talk to him about anything. He walked away from the tent feeling much better.

Avremel gave him a big welcome. "There comes our fiddler. Come in, come in."

How long before he would say: "There comes our partisan," Motele wondered. He found Avremel with an oily rag in his hand, cleaning parts of a weapon. "The innards of a Vnytovka," Avremel muttered at the shiny pieces of metal spread out before him. He looked up at his young visitor. "A weapon must be tuned up before a mission, like a fiddle before a concert."

Motele nodded, though he'd never thought of comparing a violin to a gun. A violin made music, a gun made death. The guns he had seen on the Germans, like their swastikas, always reminded him of the death of his parents and Basha. How different he felt when Yoshke's Vyntovka was pressing against him as he rode in back of him on the horse!

As if he were reading Motele's thoughts Avremel picked up the stock of the gun. He held it aloft and said, "The Avenger, that's what I call it. It's the name of every weapon in the hands of a Jewish partisan, whether it be a gun, a pistol, or a grenade. This one is particularly dear to me. I shot my first Nazi with it. I remember it to this day, bullets were flying all around me yet the words tore themselves from my throat, 'This is for my wife . . . And for my daughter, Rivkele . . . And my son, Dudek . . . And my sister, Braindel and her husband and children . . . And my father. . . .' My mother had been lucky. She died a year before the war."

"And for my father, Mendel . . . And for my mother, Dvoire . . . And for my sister, Basha . . ." he caught himself adding in his thoughts. No. He would avenge them himself. That's why he had joined the partisans. How lucky to have come in just in time to see how one tuned up a Vyntovka.

"And you," Avremel said, glancing up at Motele. "I hear you were not in a ghetto. How did you manage all this time! Were you hidden by someone?"

Motele told him of his wanderings through the villages and his various jobs. Avremel looked up again and studied his face. "I guess you could pass for a gentile boy," he finally said. "Except for the sad Jewish eyes. That's very difficult to hide."

"I didn't know my eyes looked sad," Motele said.

"Maybe that was your luck. Had you known, your eyes would have shown fear too, and there's nothing worse for a Jew trying to pass for a gentile than to give the impression he's afraid of something. Fear betrays even more than sadness. Of course, in your case it was a little different. You were born in a village and lived among gentiles all your life. But for a city Jew who lived all his life among Jews and saw a gentile once a week at the fair, when he's suddenly thrown into the gentile world he doesn't know how to behave. Take Sunday, for instance. What did you do when the peasant you lived with went to church?"

"I went to church with them," Motele said. He pressed the fingers of his right hand close together and crossed himself, saying in Ukrainian, "In the name of the Father, the Son, and the Holy Ghost."

Avremel smiled and stared at him with fascination. "The way you did it one would never say you were not a gentile. Do it again."

Motele obliged.

"And your Ukrainian!" Avremel shook his head in wonderment. "What wouldn't a Jew in the ghetto give to speak your Ukrainian. For a ghetto Jew a pure Ukrainian is like a passport to the Aryan side. That is, if he has all the other things too, such as: enough money, a good face, and the right contact to supply him with the necessary papers. Does Uncle Misha know about your Ukrainian?"

"I don't know," Motele shrugged.

"Haven't you spoken to him yet?"

"A little, in the morning."

"Then he knows. He's got a very good ear for the language, even though he himself, like most of us city Jews here, speaks it with an accent. Of course, once a Jew has made it to the forest his accent matters little. What matters is that *this* speaks without an accent," he pointed to the nearly reassembled Vyntovka. "That's why we tune up our weapons before every mission. Know any other language besides Ukrainian?"

"I speak a little Russian."

"And Yiddish, I can see, you speak like a *goy*. That's understandable. You've lived among *goyim* all your life."

Motele reddened slightly. He'd been self-conscious about his Yiddish from the moment he arrived on the base. Everyone here spoke Yiddish. It was a novel experience for him. "I was Motele only at home," he said. "Everywhere else I was Mitek."

"Well," Avremel nodded, "here you can be Motele again."

"How many languages do you speak?" Motele asked.

Avremel counted them off on his fingers: "Yiddish, which I speak like a Jew; Ukrainian, which I speak like a Jew; Russian, which I speak like a Ukrainian; and a little German that sounds like Yiddish, but good enough to fool a Ukrainian. And with the help of that little bit of German we were able to save the lives of two Jewish girls and that of a Ukrainian peasant and his family. So you see how important language can be these days. It can make a difference between life and death." He raised the now fully assembled Vyntovka, bringing it closer to the light for a final inspective look. "Well, my Avenger is ready," he said, as he placed the weapon carefully on the makeshift rack.

Motele wondered how soon the Vyntovka would see action and what the mission would be. But he was even more curious about the two girls Avremel had saved. How had he saved them, and where were they now? He hadn't seen any girls on the base. "Where are the girls now?" he asked.

"The girls?"

"The ones you said you saved."

"The two sisters, Surele and Chanele. They're in the family camp."

That family camp again. He still didn't know where it was, or what it was. All he knew was that he didn't want to go there. Not if it was not a place for real partisans who go out on missions with Avengers.

"Surele is the older one," Avremel said. "She's about fifteen now, I guess. I hear she works in the hospital. An assistant to the nurse. What the younger one does I don't know."

He tried to visualize a hospital in a forest and couldn't. Probably a hospital in name only, he thought, like what they call the kitchen here. "You didn't tell me how you saved them."

"How I saved them," Avremel said, scratching his beardless chin. He then took off his glasses, exhaled on each lens and wiped them clean with the dry rag that lay next to the oily one. When he put the glasses back on he peered at Motele as though he were testing their cleanliness on him. "It wouldn't be right to say that *I* saved them," he finally spoke, "because there were three of us. But I was the one who did all the talking since I was the one who spoke a little German.

"It all happened very fast. We received the message from our contact late in the afternoon, and that very night we acted on it. . . ."

"What's a contact?"

"A contact is a trustworthy Ukrainian who works with us. When we need some special information we contact him. And when he hears of something we should know he contacts us. In other words, he's our eyes and ears outside the forest. We have several such."

"Can a Jew also be a contact?"

"He could but it's not very likely. Remember what I told you about all the things a Jew must have to be on the Aryan side. He must have a good face, good papers, and he must speak without an accent. In your case it might be different," he studied Motele's face a moment, "you can pass for a gentile boy and your Ukrainian is perfect. And you already have experience in passing for a gentile. So I can see how you could be useful for gathering information."

"I can make believe I'm a beggar," he said eagerly, already seeing himself in the role of contact.

"A beggar?"

"Yes," Motele nodded. The truth was he hated begging, but for the partisans he would be the best beggar in the whole of the Ukraine.

"Any disguise that works is good," Avremel said. "But to come back to the story. The message from our contact was that a certain village elder, a Nazi collaborator, had somehow found out that a peasant in his village was hiding Jews and that he planned to go to Ovrutch the next day to inform the Gestapo. Now you see why we had to act fast. The Jews had to be saved that night, if they were to be saved at all. If we had known who that peasant was it would have been a simple operation. Several of us would have gone to him that night, told him he was about to be betrayed, and taken the Jews with us to the forest. But only the village elder knew who the peasant was. Even Keril, who knows everybody for miles around, didn't know."

"Who's Keril?"

"That's our contact I'm talking about. His underground name is Keril. So you see what the problem was. We couldn't very well go to that village elder and say to him, 'Tell us who that peasant is who's hiding Jews because we want to save them.' Could we?"

Motele shook his head.

"He would swear by his father and mother and the Holy Trinity that he'd never heard of such a man. And in the meantime every minute counted. So Uncle Misha hit on this idea: He called us all together and asked which of us spoke some German. Four hands went up, including my own. My pronunciation sounded better than that of the others so I was picked to be the leader. Of the other three one was to be my 'interpreter.' The other two were to be the outside guards.

"Next the four of us dressed up in German uniforms. As the leader I dressed as a lieutenant, my interpreter as a sergeant, the other two as privates. At that meeting the partisans condemned the village elder to death and I took the death warrant with me. Keril waited for us at a certain place in Klynov to take us to that village and point out to us the elder's cottage. Several partisans followed us in a horse-drawn wagon which we borrowed from a trustworthy peasant."

"Did you take your Vynovtka?" Motele asked.

"Since when are German officers armed with Russian weapons? I had a German pistol, and so did my interpreter. The guards had German rifles. Well, it was close to midnight when we knocked on his door. We got him out of bed.

" 'We heard there are some Jews hiding in your village,' I told him through my interpreter, whose Ukrainian was far from perfect but good enough for a "German," 'Do you know who the peasant is who's hiding them?'

" 'Yes, sir,' he said. 'I found out about it only today. And I want you to believe me, sir, I planned to ride into Ovrutch first thing in the morning to report to you about it.'

" 'As you see we don't wait. These *verfluchte Juden* might slip out of our hands. But don't worry,' I assured him, 'you'll get your reward just the same. Is that peasant far from here?'

" 'About five minutes ride with the auto, sir.'

" 'Our auto got stuck in the mud. We had to leave it on the road with the chauffeur.'

" 'Shall I hitch my horse to my wagon?'

" 'That won't be necessary. Just walk with us part of the way, far enough to point out the cottage. We will do the rest.'

"He got dressed quickly and before we left he told his wife to put up a samovar and set the table for a bite for the honored guests. We walked for about a quarter of an hour. 'There it is,' he said. 'The one before the last.'

" 'Now you go home,' I said, 'and wait for us.'

"We walked on by ourselves until we found the others who waited for us in the wagon. We showed them the cottage and they went in to get the Jews out while we waited outside."

"Why didn't you go in?" Motele wanted to know.

"With the German uniform on? The poor man would have been frightened to death. Even if I told him I was a Jewish partisan disguised as a German he would still think it was all a German trick. Like this it was all over in a few minutes. As soon as the wagon took off the four of us went back to the elder. We found the table laden with food and vodka and wine and, in the middle, the samovar, steaming. A regular feast. He wanted to know if we had been successful and I assured him we had. '*Alles in bester Ordnung*,' I told him. For the next few minutes I still spoke German.

"I asked him was there any other peasant in the village he suspected of hiding Jews? If so we'd go right now and take care of him and his Jews. 'No,' he said. 'I keep my eyes and ears open all the time. This is a good cooperative village. There was only this one traitor, and now we have got rid of him the village is a hundred percent pure again.'

"He gave his wife a sign and she left the room. She returned a minute later with a portrait of Adolf Hitler and hung it on the wall. 'When you knocked on the door,' he explained, 'I thought it was those bandits, the partisans, paying me a visit. I hear their favorite time is late at night. So I said to my wife, "Quick, hide the Führer under the bed. These bandits would shoot me on the spot if they saw the Führer on my wall. . . ." We are looking at a great man,' he said, lifting his eyes to the portrait. 'I look upon him as our redeemer. He will liberate us from the Bolsheviks and the Jews.'

" 'And you're not wasting any time either,' I said, lapsing into Ukrainian.

" 'Thank you,' he said, 'we all have to do our share. I see you speak Ukrainian too. And if I may say so, very well.'

" 'If you think my Ukrainian is good,' I told him, 'wait till you hear my Yiddish.'

" 'Your Yiddish!' He took it to be a joke and burst out laughing.

" '*Lach, lach, siz vey tzu dein gelechter,*' I gave him a sample of my Yiddish. He laughed until tears came to his eyes.

" 'I have great admiration for you Germans,' he said. 'You are so very, very clever. You don't miss a trick.'

" 'Wait till you see this one,' I said. I walked over to the wall, took down Hitler's portrait, and threw it to the floor. His wife let out a gasp and he stared at me in consternation. I kicked the portrait over to him and ordered him to stamp on it. 'He's your Führer,' he said.

" 'He's *your* Führer, not mine,' I told him. 'Now do as I tell you, stamp on him.'

"He didn't move. Only his eyes kept shifting from me to my partner, and back again to me, studying our faces. Then he smiled and said, 'I know what you're doing, Herr Lentnant. You're testing my loyalty to the Führer. I want to assure you I'm willing to die for him.'

" 'That privilege we will not deny you,' I told him. I ground my heels into the portrait and my partner did the same. 'This will be the fate of your redeemer,' I said, 'the enslaver of nations, the murderer of innocent people. Today we stamp on his face, tomorrow we'll dance on his grave.' Then I took the death warrant from my pocket and read it to him: 'On this day, September 23, 1943, we, Uncle Misha's Partisans, have tried you, the elder of the village, Telsk, for collaborating with the enemy and betraying the Ukrainian people. We find you guilty and condemn you to death. Sentence is to be carried out at once.' He fell to the floor and began to kiss my boots. 'Have mercy on us,' he begged. 'Take our money, our possessions, anything you wish but spare our lives.'

" 'Ask your redeemer for mercy,' I told him, 'not a partisan.'

" 'I want to live,' he whined.

" 'So did all the innocent victims you and traitors like you helped send to their death.' And with this we carried out the sentence. We left the death warrant on the table so that others would know there was a punishing hand for collaborators.''

Motele stood there, openmouthed, knowing that the story had come to an end and wishing it hadn't, wishing Avremel would go on, and on, and on, wishing that that punishing hand would reach out all the way to his own village, Stare-Mloda. The Germans were total strangers. How could they have known where the only Jewish family in Stare-Mloda lived if someone in the village had not told them, had not pointed out the house to them? Someone like this collaborator, the elder of Telsk. He hadn't been back to his village since that day he had left, because there everyone knew he was a Jew. But now he would return . . . a partisan . . . a punishing hand . . . and he himself would read the death warrant to that informer.

"Motele," Avremel broke into his reverie.

"Yes?"

"Is your fiddle tuned up?"

"I tune it up before I play."

"Here," Avremel handed him the violin case, "tune it up."

"Without notes I can only play songs," Motele explained as he was tuning up the instrument. "For serious music I need notes."

"Play a nice Yiddish *shtikele*, something that gladdens the heart."

"I only know two Yiddish songs," Motele said somewhat guiltily. " '*Oifn Pripetchik*,' and '*Lomir Sich Iberbeten*.' "

"In that case you can unload your entire Yiddish repertoire on me," Avremel said, smiling warmly at Motele.

Motele struck up "*Lomir Sich Iberbeten*" and Avremel joined in with the lyrics:

> *Lomir sich iberbeten, iberbeten,*
> *Kum aher tzu mi-ir*
> *Lomir sich iberbeten*
> *Shtey nit bei der ti-ir*

Suddenly Avremel's single voice swelled to a chorus of ten, and twenty, and fifty as the partisans, startled by the sounds of a violin in the forest, came out of their tents, abandoned their tasks and converged on the supply tent. Motele, playing outside now, swept the growing multitude with his eyes as ever more partisans crowded forward. The whole forest seemed to shake with the rising tide of their voices. And there, way in the back, he could see Yoshke, and Berek, and Uncle

Misha, the commander himself, moving their lips in unison with the others. What a thrilling sight!

On and on he played. After the Yiddish the Ukrainian, and after that the Russian, and back again to the Yiddish. And he played as never before in his life. He could feel it with every stroke of the bow, with every touch of his fingers. Oh, if only Basha could hear him now!

Basha! Basha! Can you hear me?

5 Late that afternoon the bell rang. Within minutes the partisans were assembled in front of the commander's tent, their faces grave and thoughtful. The sound of the bell at any time other than mealtimes was frequently a bad omen. Either something had happened the partisans should know about, or something was about to happen to which they should be alerted.

Motele was standing next to Avremel. Two hours earlier these same partisans had crowded around the supply tent, their eyes fixed on him as he was playing, the forest resounding with their voices. Now everyone's eyes were fixed on Uncle Misha, as they all stood in somber silence. Motele wished he were taller and didn't have to raise himself on his toes to see better. If he were standing next to Yoshke instead of Avremel, Yoshke might hoist him up on his shoulders. Better this way, he thought. He was among partisans, privileged to share their seriousness. He should be on his own feet.

"My fellow partisans," Uncle Misha began quietly, "our beloved comrade Itzik is dead."

A murmur of shock rose up from the crowd and partisans turned to each other to share their pain in silence. Itzik! their eyes seemed to say, how is that possible?

"He and his men were on the way back from a successful mission," Uncle Misha continued in the same grief-stricken voice, "when they ran into a German patrol. Our men opened fire but the Germans outnumbered them and, in addition, had a machine gun. They began to encircle our group and almost succeeded. To break through their ring of fire the machine gun had to be silenced. Itzik silenced it with his rifle. Shimon Lazar, who was close behind him, took over the gun and turned the fire on the Hitlerites. That saved the situation. One of our men, Chaim Slodkin, was severely wounded and had to be carried all the way to Klynov. Luba is with him and doing her best, but she sent word saying that Chaim must be taken to the family camp at once if he is to survive. He was badly hurt and may be in need of surgery. The others are guarding the hut where he is. I have already sent six men to relieve them.

"The problem now is getting the wounded man to the family camp. He is in no condition to ride a horse. He must be taken by wagon. This rules out our forest paths. He will have to travel on open roads. This means a possibility of running into Germans or Ukrainian police. I therefore ordered the men who left for Klynov to requisition three wagons. Because of the long journey I'm sending along a large detail of sixteen men. There's no telling what you might run into on the way. In addition to the six men in Klynov the following men will get ready to go as soon as possible." Uncle Misha took a list of names from his upper pocket and read them off.

Motele listened attentively though none of the names meant anything to him until Uncle Misha came to the last name—Yoshke. So he's going away! He wondered if Yoshke would take him along. It didn't seem likely. What would he do if they met up with Germans on the way? He had no weapon. He had never held a gun in his life. Now that he was Avremel's helper he'd probably spend his time in the supply tent sorting things. And if he was lucky, Avremel might show him how to take apart a Vyntovka, tune it up, as he said, and put it together again. His eyes scanned the crowd in a frantic search for Yoshke's face. Would he see him before he left at least? He was not yet gone and he already missed him.

"By rights," Uncle Misha continued, "Yoshke should remain on the base for a few days before going out of the forest again. He and Berek, as you know, have returned only this morning from a successful mission. The troop train they blew up carried four hundred Hitlerites in addition to weapons and equipment. But Yoshke, as an old-time coachman, knows his horses and wagons. He also knows the roads and side roads better than any of us. So he'll be in the first wagon holding the reins and the whip.

"Once you're in the wagons you'll be partisans only when you run into trouble. Otherwise you're all peasants, returning from a wedding party. When necessary you're all a little drunk. This will explain why the wounded man is lying down. He had so much of that *samagonek* he passed out. And to make the whole thing look a little more plausible our young musician, Motele, will sit up front next to Yoshke with his violin case on his lap. It's fitting to have a fiddler at a wedding party, isn't it? Your weapons will be under the straw within easy reach." Uncle Misha searched the faces in the crowd and Motele was certain he was looking for him. He raised himself up on his toes as high as he could but Uncle Misha didn't notice him. Someone else did— Yoshke. He waved to him and Motele waved back. We're going together, their hands seemed to say to each other over the crowd.

"This is all I had to tell you," Uncle Misha said. "You can go back to your tasks. And the partisans whose names I called will get ready to leave at once."

Yoshke made his way through the crowd to Motele. "Go get your fiddle, quick," he said.

"I thought I had a new helper," Avremel said, pulling Motele to himself, as though wanting to hold on to him.

"Tonight he's my helper," Yoshke said. "He's going on his first mission."

Gently Motele freed himself from Avremel's arms and ran to the supply tent for his violin. He was going on his first mission and the violin was his Vyntovka.

Basha! Basha! Can you hear me?

6 It was already dusk when the small caravan of three horse-drawn wagons started out from Klynov. All the partisans now had Ukrainian-sounding names and the proper identification papers. Motele was Mitek again. Their dress too was somewhat changed to fit the story that they were returning from a wedding party. Luba wore a white cotton-embroidered blouse and a flower-printed headkerchief tied peasant fashion under her chin. A large ivory cross, studded with red beads, hung from her neck. The men wore linen blouses with embroidered collars. This holiday attire they had borrowed from Klynov peasants.

Yoshke, who had been appointed leader of the group by Uncle Misha, sat in the driver's seat of the first wagon. Motele, his violin case wedged between his knees, sat next to him. Chaim, the wounded man, lay stretched out on a bed of straw in the second wagon. Luba, kneeling next to him, tried to make him as comfortable as possible. Someone in Yoshke's wagon said something in Yiddish and Yoshke turned around. "Since when do

Ukrainians coming home from a wedding party talk Yiddish?" he asked.

"The Jewish in-laws do," the man quipped.

They all laughed. Even the wounded man smiled.

"The truth is," one of the partisans said, "we'd be better off keeping quiet. Our blouses are Ukrainian but our tongues are tongues of city Jews."

"Except the boy," Yoshke said. "He was raised among peasants."

"Then let him be our tongue," someone suggested.

"One tongue for three wagons?" Yoshke said.

"I'll speak for the second wagon," Luba volunteered. "I may be a city Jew but it won't be the first time I pass for a country woman."

"Good," Yoshke said. "And how about the third wagon?"

There was a long silence. Finally someone said, "In the third wagon they all seem to be Jewish in-laws."

This brought a burst of laughter. "Not so loud," Yoshke warned, "you'll wake up the police."

"What do you expect from a bunch of jolly wedding guests, tears?"

"Tears?" Yoshke said, "God forbid. We've had enough tears. It's time for our enemies to cry a little." He handed the reins to Motele. "If you're going to be this wagon's tongue you might as well be the driver too. You don't need the whip. A tug on the reins is sufficient. Why hit one of God's creatures for nothing?"

Motele was thrilled to hold the reins. Knowing something about horses himself he was impressed with the way Yoshke "spoke" to the horse, the various tones he used for *"Heida," "Vyo," "Prrrrr."* In Yoshke's mouth the horse's three-word vocabulary grew into a whole language. He would try "talking" to the horse himself: *"Vyo!"* The horse picked up speed.

"Slow him down a bit," Yoshke told him. "We have a wounded man with us. The first horse sets the pace for the others."

"Prrrrr," Motele said, remembering Yoshke's tone for that word, and the horse slowed down.

"That's the way," Yoshke said, tapping Motele's back, "softly, softly. The horse has good ears."

He'd passed the test of driver! That seemed easy enough. But what about that other thing he might have to do, be the tongue for his wagon? What if he didn't say the right thing and got them all in trouble? The mere thought of it scared him. He turned to Yoshke. "What'll I tell him?"

"You've already told him," Yoshke said, "and he understood you well. He slowed down."

"I don't mean the horse. I mean the policeman."

"Well, what *would* you tell him? Let's hear."

"We're all coming home from a wedding party where I played the fiddle."

"So far so good," Yoshke said, "What else?"

"And you all got drunk."

"That's right. And you're the only sober one in the lot. And the reason for that is that you don't like that harsh *samogonka* that burns your insides. You prefer the smooth, prewar stuff that glides down your throat and warms you all over. Am I right?"

Motele laughed. The closest he ever came to an alcoholic drink were a few sips of homemade raisin wine at the Passover Seder. And even that, he remembered, went straight to his head. "And what if a German shows up?" Motele became serious again. "I can't speak German."

"If a German shows up we'll all jabber away at him," Yoshke said. "A German wouldn't know the difference between one Ukrainian accent and another. And if he tries to make trouble we'll let our weapons speak for us."

"Vyo," Motele said quietly. Just to let the horse know he was still the driver on this wagon.

Night fell. A bleak darkness descended on the countryside. The partisans sat huddled in their wagons, each with his thoughts, their silence punctured from time to time by the moaning of the wounded man. But when they passed through a village and saw the lights in the windows, and smoke curling up from the chimneys, and families gathered around tables, their thoughts turned to memories.

Once, not so long ago, they remembered, they too had enjoyed the warmth of home and the love of family. Now their homes were gone. Total strangers sat at the tables they had sat at, slept in the beds they had slept in, wore the clothes they had worn. And their families—fathers, mothers, wives, children—were all heaped in some unmarked mass grave, together with cherished dreams and cherished hopes, a bulging mound of earth the only monument to their unlived lives.

And they, the "lucky" ones, who by some miracle had managed to escape the executioner's bullet, had vowed to avenge them and destroy the destroyer of human life. Their home was the forest; the open sky their roof; their fellow partisans the only family they had; their most precious possession, their weapons. Each night, under cover of darkness, they would emerge from the forest in twos, in threes, in tens, and fan out in various directions, a silent, invisible army of Jewish fighters in search of the enemy.

The sideroads were bad—full of bumps, and ruts, and mudholes. In the dark the drivers depended more on the horses' eyes than on their own and the horses did not pick and choose. They plodded on until the wheels sank into the soft earth of a deep rut and the wagon came to a halt. "Heida! Vyo!" the drivers would shout, flicking the reins. The horses strained and pulled, the wagons creaked and the wounded man groaned in pain.

Once Luba called out, "Yoshke, have pity on Chaim. He can't take these jolts."

"Luba, I can't perform a miracle. I'm not Moses."

"Maybe take the reins from the boy."

"Even if I had two pairs of reins in my hands I couldn't do better than the boy. It's not the reins, Luba, it's the roads."

Oh, if only Basha could hear this, Motele thought. He tightened his grip on the reins and leaned forward, his eyes straining to penetrate the dark, to see what lay ahead.

What lay ahead was no improvement over what they had already passed and after a while Luba was compelled to call out again, "Yoshke, let's stop and give him a little rest. With all this jostling and shaking I can't even put the canteen to his mouth."

Yoshke told Motele to pull off the road.

As soon as her wagon came to a halt Luba adjusted Chaim's "pillow"—a sackful of straw—tucked the horse blanket carefully under him, and held the canteen to his lips for a swallow of water. "How do you feel, Chaim?" His reply was a low moan. Was he trying to tell her something? She bent over him, her ear close to his mouth. All she heard was his heavy, labored breathing. "Try to fall asleep, Chaim. Sleep is the best medicine for you now," Luba whispered. She wondered whether he had even understood what she said. She waited a while longer and then got off the wagon to join the others.

The moon had come up, but it was a pale sliver be- set by tatters of drifting cloud that kept hiding even the little light it had to offer. They moved off the road and sat down in the field in a close circle, as they did in the forest to hear Uncle Misha's reports. What was lacking now was the campfire they had nightly at the base.

"First let's hear what our nurse has to say," Yoshke proposed.

"If you don't mind, Yoshke, I'll speak as Luba, not as 'our nurse.' That title was bestowed on me only because I'm a woman, the only woman in the detachment. Giving a wounded man a sip of water doesn't make one a nurse. But as Luba I can tell you this: If we don't get to that family camp very soon we're bound to lose our comrade Chaim before we get there. With luck, only a doctor could save him, perhaps."

"If we continue on these sideroads," Yoshke told them, "we'll be lucky if we make it in four hours."

"And what if we switch to the main road?" someone asked.

"By the main road we could probably cut the time in half. But there we're bound to run into a German patrol, you know the Germans search every wagon that comes their way. If that should happen they'll get their hands on our weapons before we do and Chaim will be the first casualty because he's completely helpless."

"To be frank with you," Luba said, "I doubt if he could last even two hours without medical help."

The partisans fell silent, pondering their dilemma.

Motele, who had listened carefully to everything that was said, also had something to say but hesitated. What could he, a twelve-year-old, tell these old experienced partisans that they didn't already know? Yoshke, he knew, wouldn't laugh if he made a fool of himself, but the others might. But wasn't he one of them, picked by Uncle Misha himself? And if so, wasn't it his duty to speak up if he had something to say? "Yoshke," he said, in a quavering voice, glad they couldn't see the red on his face.

"Yes, Motele?"

"I was just thinking. . . . In the village next to Stare-Mloda, where I used to live, there lived an old Ukrainian doctor, a city doctor who settled in the country. When I or my sister, Basha, got sick my father went for him in our wagon. He didn't want to take any money so my father paid him in flour. I know his house. . . ."

There was silence but no laughter. After a long pause one of the partisans said, "Stare-Mloda? Where is that? How far from here?"

Motele was about to say something but Yoshke spoke for him: "Stare-Mloda is quite a ways from here," he said. "It lies in another direction altogether."

"Then the whole thing is out of the question," someone said.

"Stare-Mloda may be out of the question," Luba spoke up, "but the boy's suggestion is worth giving a thought to. If we can't get Chaim to a doctor, we should perhaps consider the idea of how to bring a doctor to Chaim."

"Here? In the dark? In the middle of nowhere? Even if we succeed in getting a doctor what could he do, operate on a wagon of straw?"

"Who says it has to be here, in the dark, in the middle of nowhere?" Luba said, calmly. "We're only a few kilometers from the next village. As soon as we get there we stop being Ukrainian wedding guests and become Uncle Misha's partisans again. We knock on the door of the first hut with a light on and tell the peasant we need a bed, even if it has to be his own. If he's a friendly peasant and cooperates, so much the better. If he's not, we do what we always do, we take it. Our comrade, Chaim, got wounded fighting his enemy too, not only ours."

"So we get him into a hut," someone said. "And then what?"

"Then we see what we can do about a doctor. The peasant himself may be able to help us. He knows this area and we don't. In the meantime Chaim is on a bed in a warm hut and not on a heap of straw out in the cold."

"I think we all agree that Luba's plan is a sensible one," Yoshke said.

"Please don't say Luba's plan," Luba protested. "It's really the boy's idea."

"The boy has a name," Yoshke said. "Motele. And

if he's a fiddler coming home from a Ukrainian wedding party he's Mitek."

"I like Motele better," Luba said.

"You missed a good concert this afternoon, Luba," someone called out.

"A concert! The very word now sounds strange to my ears. A word from another world. And I used to go to concerts every week. Well, as soon as we get Chaim taken care of I'm going to claim what I missed. And I'll insist on the same program." She rose to her feet and the others did the same. On the way back to their wagons Luba caught up with Motele, put her arm around him and kissed him on the cheek. He felt as though his face were aflame with heat. For the second time that night he was glad it was dark and no one could see him blush.

At first glance there was not a sign of life in the village, but as they looked about them more carefully they discovered two huts that showed some light through their shuttered windows. Tacked on to the lone lamp-post was a wooden sign that said: KRASNY. The name didn't tell them anything. Nor could they know from the outside of the two lighted huts whether the peasants inside them were friendly or hostile to partisans. And since one could be as good or as bad as the other they decided to take their chances in the first.

They fished out their weapons from under the straw and in that instant they became partisans again. With catlike silence they climbed out of the wagons and surrounded Yoshke who whispered his instructions. Three were to remain with the wounded man. Two were to take up posts at the village entrance. Five were to surround the hut and the rest were to enter it. Luba thought she should remain behind near Chaim but Yoshke insisted that she come inside to pick the right bed.

Standing near Yoshke and being left out from the instructions Motele felt useless and embarrassed. Here he was with Uncle Misha's partisans getting ready for action, and he was holding a violin case in his hand. They had all ceased being wedding guests and he was the wedding musician. He kept looking at Yoshke hoping to be noticed, but Yoshke was busy picking the men for their assigned posts. When the last man had been picked Motele was certain he had been forgotten. But to his surprise he heard Yoshke say, "As for Motele— where is he?"

"Here I am!" Motele called out. In his excitement he forgot he was supposed to whisper.

"Shshsh," Yoshke admonished him, "you'll wake up the village."

Of all the times to be stupid he had to pick this one! "I'm sorry," he whispered.

"For you I have a special job," Yoshke said. "You'll be our messenger. That's the first time we'll have such a luxury. You'll be with me in case I have to send out word to the others. But a messenger has to be able to run and you're bound to trip over your fiddle. Put it back in the wagon. No one will steal it."

The men scattered to their assigned places. Motele was amazed at how quickly and noiselessly they had vanished, all except the three who were to guard the wounded man. They wore boots and moved as though they were barefoot. Only those who were to enter the hut now clustered around Yoshke for final instructions. Motele stood close to him, straining to hear every whispered word. "You, Luba, will knock on the door. At this hour they'll probably not open until they know who it is. You'll tell them you got lost and need directions. A woman's voice is not bound to arouse suspicion. Once they open a crack my foot will be in the door."

"If I may suggest, Yoshke, not only should I knock but at first just I and the boy should go in. I and my little brother, Mitek."

"What's the point in that?" Yoshke wanted to know. "We're partisans now and not wedding guests."

"The point is," Luba explained, "we're looking for a bed for Chaim. But supposing we don't find what we're looking for?"

"Even the poorest peasant has a bed, Luba. And we've decided not to stand on ceremony and take it for Chaim. So why delay?"

"But what if the bed happens to be occupied by a

woman in labor? Or by a man with a communicable disease, like tuberculosis? Do we want to put Chaim in such a bed?"

"And you say you're not a nurse, Luba. Who but a good nurse would think of such precautions? All right. Supposing the bed is not for Chaim?"

"So I thank them for the "directions," say good-night and we go to the next hut without leaving a trail behind us. And if I find the right bed I'll send our messenger for you."

"You've convinced me, Luba. And you and Mitek are still wedding guests," he added, chuckling.

"For a few more minutes at least," she said. "But I'd better look like one." She snapped off the leather cartridge belt she had put on only a while ago, took the pistol out of the holster and stuck it in her jacket pocket, and carried the belt back to the wagon. Then she pulled the cross out over her jacket and said, "Now we can go."

As they were crossing the road Motele became aware of the sound of footsteps. He lifted his feet higher and put them down lightly, the soles of his boots barely touching the ground.

As they approached the fence Luba whispered, "Looks more like a house than a hut. A porch . . . wide windows . . . shingled roof. . . ."

"Could be a wealthy peasant," Yoshke guessed.

"Or the village elder," Luba said.

Motele remembered the village elder in Avremel's

story and wondered whether they would find a picture of Hitler hanging on the wall. If Luba and Yoshke stamp on it he'd make sure to add his foot. He watched Yoshke pull back the latch on the fence gate so quietly it didn't click. "I'll be leaning against the house," he heard him whisper to Luba before he disappeared.

Motele kept close to Luba when she knocked on the door. His heart beat loudly, as though it echoed Luba's knock. "I must remember I'm her brother," he told himself, "and I'm Mitek again." He'd been Motele so many times that day he was afraid he might forget himself. It didn't take long before a woman's voice called out from the other side of the door, "Stashu?"

"Luba Pochlowitcha," Luba said, slurring over the name.

There was a long pause before the voice was heard again, "What do you want?"

"I'm a stranger. I lost my way. Could you help me please?"

Cautiously the woman opened the door a crack and peered suspiciously over Luba's shoulder.

"This is my little brother," Luba said, pulling Motele closer to her. "Say good evening to the lady, Mitek."

"Good evening, ma'am."

"This your wagon out there?"

"Yes," Luba said. "And my uncle is on it, sound asleep. A little too much samogonka," she chuckled. "We've been to a wedding, you see. A relative. He couldn't even hold the reins. I had to take them and lost my way."

"Where are you heading for?"

"In the vicinity of Ovrutch," Luba said. "And I was doing well until I got off the main road. Now I don't know how to get back on it again."

"Ovrutch! Good Lord! You have a long ways to go yet. My husband is the one to tell you the quickest way to get there. He often goes there on business. He should be home soon." She hesitated a moment. "I guess you might as well wait for him inside," she finally said.

"Thank you," Luba said, taking Motele's hand.

As soon as they entered the room Motele scanned the walls for Hitler's picture. There wasn't any. Instead he saw hanging on a wall something he'd seen in every peasant hut he'd been to, a large wooden icon—Jesus bleeding on the cross, a crown of thorns on his head. But he could see at a glance this was no peasant hut. It was crammed with furniture, and city furniture at that. Everywhere you turned there was something standing next to something. Brown polished chairs wedged in between china closets with fancy carvings and glass doors; small, round-topped tables with lamps on them wedged in between chairs. There was hardly an inch of empty wall space left. And in the center of the room stood a large mahogany table, the carvings at the end of the legs resembling a lion's claws. It reminded him of the table in his violin teacher's living room. He caught a glimpse of the woman watching Luba as she was scanning the room, and seemed pleased with Luba's interest in what she was seeing. "Have a seat," she said, with a grand sweep of the arm. There was no dearth of chairs.

"Thank you," Luba said. She picked one of the straight-backed chairs at the table, and Motele sank into a black, leather-covered armchair.

"I have been admiring your furniture," Luba said. "You have very good taste, if I may say so."

"It's my husband who deserves the credit. I just keep it nice and shiny. It can keep you busy all day long."

City furniture and peasant Ukrainian, Motele thought as he listened to the woman's speech. He hadn't been aware of these things until today when first Avremel and later Yoshke spoke about the importance of the right accent at certain times. "It could make a difference between life and death," he remembered Avremel saying. Luba's accent was not bad, for a city Jew that is. But since they all said his was perfect, perhaps he should talk up, say something just so the woman would hear his speech. "What kind of business is your husband in?" he blurted out before he could change his mind.

"What makes you think he's in business?" the woman said, smiling at him.

"You said he often goes to Ovrutch on business."

"I should have said *official* business. My husband is Captain of Police in this district. When he goes to Ovrutch it's on official business."

Motele gulped and felt the opposite of blushing. He felt as though all the color had gone out of his face and he was as pale as a ghost. He was glad the woman had turned to Luba.

"At least twice a week my husband says to me, 'Katiushka, don't count on me being home for supper. I'll be going to Ovrutch on official business.' If it's just to report to the Herr Kommandant he returns that same day, late at night. But if it's on ghetto business he's sometimes away for days. But he never comes back empty-handed. In the beginning, when they pushed them into the ghettos he'd bring home furniture. As captain he got the better pieces. All these things you see here," she made a sweep of the hand around the room, "that's Jew furniture. Now they're cleaning them out of the ghettos. Getting rid of them for good. Now he brings home clothes. The Germans let my husband take some of the better things. The cheaper things they give to the peasants, their reward for digging the pits. Come, I'll show you some of my things."

Luba didn't move. It was as though she hadn't heard the woman's last words. She sat there staring at the woman, her pale face, paler than Motele's own had felt a minute ago.

"Aren't you curious?" the woman said, her hand reaching out for Luba's.

Rather than be touched by this woman, Luba rose on her own. She turned to Motele. "Go out and see if Uncle woke up. You heard what the lady said. The captain will be home soon." With her back to the woman she managed a quick wink and Motele replied with a nod and left. Luba followed the woman out of the room. The woman paused in front of a closed door and, pointing to it with a tilt of her head, said, "That's the children's bedroom. My two little angels are sleeping there. Girls. One six and one eight." She went on to the next door and opened it. "Our bedroom," she said proudly. "The best in Jew furniture," she added with a laugh.

This room too was crowded with possessions—two three-quarter beds separated by a night table, a chair on either side of the beds, a dresser, a chest of drawers, two clothes closets, one next to the other, nearly filling the entire width of a wall. And hanging over the beds was another icon, smaller than the one in the main room but showing the same pained and suffering Jesus.

"I'll show you what's in the closet," the woman said, turning the key in the closet door. "The other closet is my husband's." She took a black velvet dress off the hanger and held it up against herself. "This one I didn't have to fix. It fitted just right. But some of the others, like this one for instance . . ." she laid the velvet dress on the bed and now measured the second one for length against herself, "I had to work on quite a lot."

And so the comments went with each dress she took out. This one had fitted perfectly and that one had to be shortened, or widened, or let out at the hem. This one was her favorite, and that one she wore to a wedding recently.

Luba felt herself growing faint. To each dress the woman took out of the closet she added a body, a head, a face. Relatives. Friends. Acquaintances. Women she had known and loved—they were lying motionless now. Heaped one on top of the other—the pit! She had escaped from the ghetto in time to escape the pit and had come upon it a full year later, here in this Ukrainian village. . . .

The woman chattered on but all that Luba heard was the drone of her voice. She seemed caught in a macabre partnership with this stranger. For every dress the woman brought out she had to find a body. There must be no bodyless dress on that bed, in that pit. And there was no end to the dresses, and no end to the women. . . .

She wanted to cry out, "Stop!" but she seemed to have lost her speech. She wanted to reach out for the woman's throat and strangle her and toss her, lifeless, on the heap with the others but her hands seemed to be paralyzed. She was numb with grief.

"And what do you say to this one?" the woman held

up a long white satin dress, turning it slowly for Luba to see the back as well as the front.

Luba stared at it, her eyes brimming with tears. "Tanya!" she gasped. "Tanya's wedding dress."

"Who on earth is Tanya?" the woman said.

"My sister-in-law in the Sernik ghetto."

The woman's eyes went from Luba's face to the cross and back again to her face, as though she were trying to match the two. "So you had a Jew in the family," she said coldly. "Your brother was married to a Jew."

"Yes. He was married to a Jew."

"But he didn't have to go to the ghetto."

"He had to."

"He wanted to?"

"Nobody wanted to. They took him. And they took my two older sisters, and my father, and my mother, and our uncles, and cousins, and nieces, and nephews. The whole family."

"Then you were all Jews."

"You figured it out, at last. Yes, we were all Jews."

"How come . . .?"

"You mean how come I'm alive and not with the others in that pit your husband helped dig? I'll tell you why. I had a special reason to stay alive. I had to know whether Tanya's wedding dress would fit you perfectly, or whether you'd have to make some alterations."

"You get out of my house, you Jewish scum. If my husband catches you here you *will* be joining the others, believe me."

"You don't have enough yet in that closet? You think this will enrich your wardrobe?" Luba pointed to her leather jacket.

"Get out! Get out!" the woman shouted.

"You'll wake up your two little angels."

"Don't you worry about my two little angels." She put the dress down on the bed and folded her arms over her chest. "Now, are you getting out or do I have to throw you out?"

"I prefer that you throw me out," Luba said, pulling the pistol from her pocket and aiming it at the woman.

Frightened, the woman backed away, stepping backward till she was stopped by the wall. "You want your sister-in-law's dress, take it. Take it and go."

"I want my sister-in-law. I want my brother. I want my entire family your husband handed over to the German executioners. Give me them and I'll go."

"You blame my husband for what the Germans did. I know my husband. He's a good man. They force him to do things he doesn't like to do. Everytime he comes home from one of those ghetto jobs he's so upset he can't sleep for nights."

"Yes, I'm sure he comes home loaded down with remorse—and rewards. Dresses, suits, furniture, jewelry—how about jewelry? Rings . . . watches . . . the Germans like to get their hands on them first, but your husband certainly deserves a gold watch or two."

"So it's jewelry you want. Then why don't you say so. I have a little and I'll give you some. I'll give you a nice ladies' gold watch and gold ring, and the dress, if you promise to go." She started walking forward but Luba stopped her. "Stay where you are," she said, shaking the gun at her.

"I was going for the jewelry," she said. "It's right there," she pointed to the night table between the beds and began to advance again.

"Stay where you are, I said," Luba warned sternly. With three quick steps she was at the night table. She pulled open the drawer. A shiny German Luger was all that was there. Luba took out the pistol and stuck it in her pocket.

"My husband's," the woman said, defiantly. "He's a policeman. He's never without his gun."

"You husband will never again aim a gun at a Jew, or anybody else for that matter. This much I can assure you."

The woman pulled a gold ring off her finger. "Here, take it," she said, "take it and the dress, and a few more dresses if you want, and go. If my husband comes it'll be too late." There were sounds of the door slamming shut and of footsteps. "There he comes now!" she cried out jubilantly. "Stashu! Stashu! Quick, here I am!"

Yoshke appeared in the bedroom doorway. Motele and two more partisans were right behind him. "There's no need for a bed anymore, Luba," Yoshke said, somberly.

Luba stared at him in disbelief, then put the pistol in her pocket and wiped her eyes with the back of her hand. "When did it happen?" she said, in a barely audible voice.

"Just a few minutes ago. He'd started to say something to the men by the wagon, but they couldn't understand him. One of the men ran over to call me and by the time I reached the wagon he was gone."

"Chaim. Our dear, beloved Chaim," she muttered. She swayed, as though her feet were giving way. Yoshke took her by the arm and led her into the living room. One of the partisans pushed a chair under her, another fetched a glass of water. The woman had in the meantime come out of the bedroom and was heading for the door.

"She's going out," Motele alerted Yoshke.

"Let her. She won't get very far."

A minute later she returned to the room wringing her hands and whimpering. "They won't let me out of the house," she said to the partisan standing behind Yoshke. The man looked at her impassively and shrugged. The man behind Luba was scanning the room, his eyes moving from one piece of furniture to the next. No one, it seemed to Motele, was paying any attention to the woman except him. He watched her leave the room again, heading for the bedroom. He was a few steps behind her. The closet was still open, still half-full. She bypassed it and went straight to the window. Slowly she began pulling up the bottom half. A hand outside slammed it shut. She sat down on the bed, buried her face in her hands and cried. Motele went back to the living room. Luba too was crying. Two women in tears. Two different kinds of sorrow.

"Luba," Yoshke said, putting his hand on hers, "we must make some decisions."

"Yes, Yoshke, I'm listening." She wiped her eyes dry and leaned forward.

"That captain—I propose that instead of meting out partisan justice on the spot, we take him back to the base. He might be a valuable tongue."

"I agree," Luba nodded.

"And what about her?"

"She has two kids," Luba said, after a pause.

"And this?" Yoshke said, pointing to the furniture.

"We should do what the Jews of Lachwa did when the Germans and their fascist Ukrainian helpers came to liquidate the ghetto. They set the houses on fire so not a single one of their possessions would fall into the hands of the murderers. But that heapful of dresses you saw on the bed, that we should take for the women in the family camp. I'll keep just one," she added quietly, "my sister-in-law's wedding dress."

"You recognized it."

Luba nodded. "Like all women in the ghetto she bartered away her garments one after the other, for a piece of bread for the children, but held on to this one. Every woman tried to hold on to one decent dress for as long as she could. If you look, Yoshke, you too may recognize something."

"I won't," Yoshke shook his head determinedly. "And I don't think you should look at them again. And I don't think we should take them to the family camp. For just that reason. Someone is bound to recognize something. Let these dresses go up in flames together with all this," his hand swept around the room to indicate the furniture. Let them mingle into one big flame that will light up the heavens. . . ." He was interrupted by the sounds of a scuffle outside the house. "They have him," he said, rising to his feet. Luba too was on her feet. They stood there, listening. Presently the sounds died down and the door was pushed open. The captain, already disarmed and hatless, was brought in by two partisans. He was still panting from the struggle, his big frame heaving with each breath he took. His wife burst into the room. "Stashu!" she cried.

The two stared at each other in silence. "Who are they? What are they doing here?" he finally demanded, his voice ringing with accusation.

"It's this one," she whimpered, pointing to Luba. "She tricked me into opening the door."

He looked at Luba and then at the others. They all

had their hands on their weapons and he was weapon-less. Frustration and defeat were stamped on his face.

"If your wife doesn't know who we are then I'll tell you," Yoshke said. "We are Uncle Misha's partisans. All Jews. Jews you didn't drag to the pits."

"I have not harmed any Jews. Whoever told you that lied to you."

"That's why the Germans rewarded you with all this," Yoshke said, indicating the furniture, "for your kindness to Jews."

"Tell him how he got this furniture," Luba said to the woman. "And the dresses. Tell him what you told me."

"She tricked me, Stashu," the woman said, "she tricked me with her cross."

"Shut your mouth, idiot!" the officer shouted at his wife. He turned to Yoshke. "Take it . . . the furniture . . . the dresses . . . everything. And, to show that I want to make a clean breast of it, the money too. Every last ruble. It's yours." He took a step forward but the two partisans held him back. He turned to one of the partisans who held his arm. "I'm not trying to escape," he said, smiling weakly. "I'm just going to the bedroom to get the money."

"Stashu," his wife whimpered.

"Shut up! Idiot!"

"She only wants to save you a trip, captain," Luba said. "We already have the 'money' you so generously want to give us." She took the Luger out of her pocket. "Isn't this it? With your wife it was the jewelry. With you it's the money."

He lowered his head. Motele expected him to fall at Yoshke's feet and beg for his life, as the village elder had done in Avremel's story. But the man didn't move, nor look at anyone. When he finally lifted his head he said to Yoshke, "I'm a father of two children."

"The pits are filled with fathers and children," Yoshke said.

"You will shoot me."

"You will get partisan justice." And to the two men who held his arms Yoshke said, "Take him out and put him on the third wagon."

"Stashu!" the woman cried as they led him away.

He didn't look back. It was as though he held her responsible too for his fate. She tried to run after him but one of the partisans stopped her at the doorway.

"You better take your two little angels and run from here," Luba said to the woman. "This house is going up in flames."

The woman stared vacantly at Luba, as though the warning was beyond her understanding. She stood there, in the middle of the room, wringing her hands and muttering *"Hospodi! Hospodi!"* "My God, my God," while the partisans went about their task of setting the house on fire. One of them let the animals out of the barn and then put a match to the hay. Another brought a heap of straw into the room and they each took fistfuls of it and scattered it under and around the furniture. They moved swiftly and efficiently. It was not the first time that they had set a collaborator's house on fire. In the end it was Luba who had to rouse the woman from her stupor and push her and the children out into the night.

"Jews, let us say Kaddish," Yoshke said, leaning his head against the middle wagon. Quickly the other partisans gathered around him. And while Luba and Motele guarded their prisoner, Yoshke, a humble coachman who had never led a congregation in prayer, now led his fellow partisans in the prayer for the dead—"*Yisgadal veyiskadash shmey rabo . . .*" they chanted the Hebrew words in unison. Then they climbed into the wagons and took off. This time they held their weapons at the ready. They were no longer Ukrainians coming from a wedding party. They were Uncle Misha's partisans returning from a mission.

7 Motele opened his eyes and found himself in a tent; but a tent made of canvas and not the kind he knew at the partisan base. And he was on a regular cot and not on a heap of straw on the ground. And it was not Luba who was standing near him but a girl he had never seen before. Where was he? he wondered. Had he been captured? Had he fallen into enemy hands?

"Good morning," the girl said in Yiddish. "I thought you'd never wake up."

The sound of the language gave him his life back. He noticed the thermometer in her hand and surmised he was in the family camp hospital. But he had no recollection of how he got here and when. He was about to ask when she stuck the thermometer in his mouth and silenced him. There was nothing about her dress to indicate she was a nurse. Since when do nurses wear leather jackets and berets? It was the way she held his wrist and concentrated on his pulsebeat that made him feel he was in good hands. He had no way of guessing her age except that she was younger looking than Luba. But Luba, he thought, was prettier.

He suddenly remembered the violin. His eyes searched the tent. There was no sign of the instrument. He was about to talk with the thermometer in his mouth but didn't. And when she finally took it out he waited till she finished reading it. "Normal," she said, her face, serious until now, broke into a smile. "Perfectly normal."

"Where's my violin?" he demanded.

"I tell him he's normal and all he can think of is the violin. A true artist. Have no worries. Your violin is safe. It's in Commander Zissman's tent." She shook the thermometer down, wiped it and put it back in its case. "How about some breakfast?" she asked.

The thought of black chicory did not seem very appealing to him at that moment but his parched throat and dry mouth thirsted for some liquid, any liquid. So he said, "Yes, please," and added, "The canteen is in my coat pocket."

"I'm afraid you'll have to drink from a glass," she told him. "Besides, your coat isn't even here. It's in the laundry with the rest of your clothes. That's the rule here. When a partisan is admitted to the hospital his clothes are taken away for washing and repairing. When he comes out he not only feels better, he also feels cleaner."

They're treating me like a real partisan, he thought with satisfaction. And he'd been on only one mission.

That was more than two months ago. Did he really deserve that title?

As far as he was concerned he was still a partisan in name only. He had been luckiest on his first day at Uncle Misha's base. Everything exciting had happened that day—from Yoshke's and Berek's discovery of him in the field to going on his first and only mission, ending with the capture of the Ukrainian police captain. Since then he had not ventured out of the base except to take the horses out to the field for grazing. The rest of the time he was Avremel's helper. But always it was other partisans who rode out on the horses he cared for; and it was other partisans who used the weapons he cleaned and oiled.

"Be patient, Motele," Yoshke would tell him whenever he asked to be taken along on a mission. "Your day will come." His day had come, indeed. On a hospital cot! And with Yoshke nowhere in sight.

"How long do you think I'll have to be here?" he said to the nurse.

"If your temperature remains normal for the next two days Dr. Kluger will probably discharge you from here. I'd never have thought you would recover that fast. You had 104° when they brought you in."

They? He had no recollection of the trip, or of who it was that brought him here. All he remembered now was Luba bending over him, holding a cold compress to his forehead, while he, wrapped in blankets, was shivering. "Do you know who brought me here?" he asked.

"I wasn't on duty then but I was told it was a man and a woman. The woman is probably Luba. I've met her a number of times. She always brings the wounded from Uncle Misha's camp."

"Then the man was Yoshke," he said with certainty.

"I don't know a Yoshke. But I know a partisan in your camp named Avremel. Do you know him?"

"I do," Motele nodded. "I'm his helper."

"You are!" her words rang with the joy of discovery. "How is he?" she said eagerly, "tell me." She sat down on the edge of the cot, looking at him expectantly.

"He's fine," Motele said, and at that moment he knew who the nurse was. "You have a younger sister, haven't you?"

"Yes. Chanele. How do you know?"

"Avremel told me how he saved the lives of two sisters and that one of them is a nurse in the family camp."

"That's me, Surele. What's your name?"

"On a mission I'm Mitek but on the base I'm Motele."

"Motele!" she beamed at him, as though she had discovered a long lost friend. "Oh, wait till Chanele hears this." She leaned over and took his hand in hers. "You say you're Avremel's helper. What is he doing?"

"He's in charge of the supply tent. We sort out the uniforms and keep the weapons in good condition. I can take apart a Vyntovka, clean it, oil it, and put it together again." Having boasted, he was glad she didn't ask him whether he'd actually used one. One day soon he would, he told himself. He wouldn't consider himself a full-fledged partisan before he used a Vyntovka. Just thinking about it made him eager for action. "What's the matter with me?" he said. "Why am I here?"

"You probably had a mild case of forest. But you're all right now," she added reassuringly.

"Of forest?" He'd never heard of an illness by that name.

"The forest can both heal you and make you sick. Some partisans had illnesses for years that disappeared in the forest. Nobody knows why. It's a mystery. And some, who had never been sick, got what you just had, an attack of high fever and the shivers. And that's also a mystery. But we'll take good care of you here," she said, squeezing his hand as she rose, "and in no time you'll be on your feet again. If Dr. Kluger should come by tell him I went for your breakfast." She waved to him before she stepped out of the tent.

Alone now he surveyed the tent carefully and for the first time noticed the empty cot along the canvas wall, all made up, ready for occupancy; the big barrel on top of which stood several medicine bottles and jars bulging with cotton; the two wooden horses and, leaning against them, a broad board, which he surmised could instantly be turned into an operating table. And there was the large kerosene lamp hanging from the center of the tent that provided the light.

It seemed strange to find these things in the depth of a forest. Especially the clean white pillow cases. At Uncle Misha's base the partisans flop down on a heap of straw and use their own folded coats for pillows. But then again, if they can have a laundry and a tailor shop in the forest, why not cots with pillows in white cases?

He bent over to look under the cot. They had taken his clothes but left his boots that were at least two sizes too large. His feet were swimming in them. Avremel had given him a choice: A pair of boots taken off a dead Fritz that were comfortable though not a perfect fit, and these that had once belonged to a Russian soldier. He took one look at the swastika stamped inside the Fritz's boots and chose the Russian's. If they have a shoemaker here, he thought, maybe he could do something with these boots. He would ask Surele when she got back. Might as well have everything done at once.

He leaned back. His body ached to be horizontal. His head was drawn to the pillow. Only now did he realize how weak this mild case of "forest" had left him. Despite Surele's reassuring words he was terribly discouraged because he felt helpless, physically helpless. Hardly the condition for a partisan to be in.

"Basha," he heard himself whisper. He knew she had not the power to make his wishes come true. But it was such a comfort to talk to her, to let her know how he felt, to be assured by her that all will be well. "Basha, do you hear me?"

He was waiting for her response when the tent flaps parted and a tall man, bending low, entered head first. The Commander! Motele thought when he spotted the pistol protruding from the man's holster. "Good morning," the man's booming voice filled the tent.

"Good morning," Motele replied, trying to sound a little more vigorous than he was.

"Where is the nurse?"

"She went to get me breakfast."

"How's your appetite this morning?" the man said, approaching the cot.

At that moment Motele hadn't the slightest desire for food. "Good," he said, and was instantly betrayed by a sudden rush of heat to his face. To his surprise the man reached for his wrist. "Are you the doctor?" Motele looked up at the bearded face towering over him.

The man nodded, concentrating on his pulsebeat. "Normal," was the verdict when he released the wrist. "I assume the nurse has taken your temperature and found it normal. Otherwise she wouldn't have gone for your breakfast."

"Yes. It's normal."

"If there's no change in temperature in the next two days you'll be out of here."

"Out of the camp?"

"Out of the hospital. I'll tell Commander Zissman to give you some light work in the beginning, until you get your strength back." And with that the doctor strode out of the tent.

In the beginning. How long will that beginning last and what will come after it? Why couldn't he do some light work at Uncle Misha's base until he got his strength back? What could be lighter than oiling a Vyntovka or leading horses out to the field? In less than five minutes the doctor had both given him his freedom and clamped a prison sentence on him. He was so agitated he could have cried. "Basha, Basha, did you hear what he said?"

Laughter and a babble of young voices burst upon him. The forest magnified sounds, giving them a sharp clarity. He held his breath, listening. Stillness again. Forest stillness. Then he saw a tray. Behind it, its bearer, Surele. And behind her, following with timid steps, a girl whose appearance startled him. It was as though Basha had answered his call in person. The round face, large, dark eyes, the hair parted in the middle, the long braids, hanging down almost to arm's length—Basha!

"This is my sister, Chanele," the nurse said, holding on to the tray till he gripped it with both hands. "I told her you knew Avremel so she wanted to meet you."

The girl smiled at him and, as if to round out the resemblance, her smile too reminded him of his sister. It was a full-faced smile that lighted up the eyes as well. "Hello," she nodded.

"Hello," he replied, blushing slightly and wishing she wouldn't stare at him so intently. To break the awkward silence he thought of something to say to Surele: "The doctor was here and he took my pulse."

"And it was normal, and in two days you may be discharged from here."

"How do you know?"

"He told me. He came to the kitchen and ordered two rolls for you instead of one. He said your appetite was good, you told him. And that's a good sign."

He looked at the tray in front of him. A glass of warm milk and two buttered rolls. He didn't have the appetite for one and now he would have to eat both. He would force himself to if necessary. "Yes, I told him so."

"Now *I'm* going to have breakfast," Surele announced. "Chanele, you keep our partisan company till he's finished. And you'll bring the tray back to the kitchen. Good appetite, Motele," she said as she left the tent.

There was no delaying any longer. Appetite or no, he had to come to grips with these two large rolls. He took a sip of the milk first. The warm, smooth, velvety liquid lubricated his parched throat and brought back a taste he'd almost forgotten. At home, before the war, he and Basha had just such a breakfast each morning before going off to school. The milk came from a peasant nearby who brought it fresh from the udder, and the rolls were from their own oven.

"This milk is from our own cows," Chanele said, as though reading his thoughts.

"You have a farm here?"

"We have cows for milking and cows for slaughtering

and some goats too for those who need goats' milk. One of our partisan details is always out, roaming the villages for food supplies. That's in addition to what other partisan detachments give us. We have over sixteen hundred people to feed."

He told her he knew how partisans got their provisions. Some peasants gave willingly, others had to be coerced. He himself had not yet been on such a mission, he said. But his friend Yoshke had. Many times.

The sharp metallic clang of steel on steel was suddenly heard.

"Is this the call for breakfast?" Motele asked.

"No," Chanele said, laughing. "That's Feivish, the blacksmith, shoeing horses. He's quite a distance from here but the forest carries sounds. You'll get used to it."

"You have a blacksmith here? In the forest?"

"Are you surprised? We even have a kind of steambath. And on the Sabbath you can see the religious Jews hurrying to *shul* to *dahvn*."

"You have a shul too?" he stared at her in surprise.

"One day a week one of the tents becomes a shul. This camp is called 'the Jerusalem of the Forest.'"

He'd finished the first roll and found appetite to bite into the second. And he hadn't blushed even once since he was alone with her! Was it because she reminded him so much of his sister?

"I work in the kitchen," Chanele volunteered.

"As soon as I get well I go back to Uncle Misha's base. I may soon go on a mission. I know the Vyntovka inside out."

"All my friends talked about you," she said after a long silence.

He seemed surprised. "I've been on only one mission," he said.

"About your being a musician, I mean. Aren't you a violinist?"

"Yes, but I'm a partisan first."

"We were hoping you'd play at one of our campfires."

"If there's time. The commander has my violin."

"Yes. We heard. Oh," she clasped her hands excitedly, "it'll be the first time that we've had a violinist. We have someone who plays the harmonica. Not bad. But a violin.... Do you know 'Partizaner Lid'?"

He shook his head.

"It's a partisan song. We sing it at all the campfires. It's the most popular song in camp." She began to hum the tune.

"Nice melody."

"I'll teach you," she said eagerly.

8 His clothes had been mended and washed, and his large boots exchanged for a smaller-sized pair that fitted. His coat was shortened somewhat, and he now had a button for every buttonhole. The buttons didn't match, but what did it matter? He was free of the rope which made him look like a beggar. But best of all he had Chanele, his friend, his guide around camp, with whom he spent every free moment she had.

A whole week had passed since he'd been discharged from the hospital tent and was assigned to a tent for two with a sixteen-year-old youth named Shloime, a mechanic's apprentice at the camp's general repair shop. Throughout this time he'd not heard from Yoshke once and he was beginning to wonder why, and if he'd ever see him again. With partisans one could never tell. Both cots in the hospital tent were now occupied by wounded partisans, one of whom, he'd heard from Surele, was hovering between life and death.

If someone would at least tell him something about his status in this camp. Was he here for good, or on a temporary basis? The only person who would know was Commander Zissman and he was away on a food-gathering mission, which always took longer than a combat mission. If only he had something to do in the meantime. He'd persuaded Shloime to take him along to the repair shop. That was the kind of a job he would like if he had to stay here awhile. He could then become Berek's assistant after he got back to Uncle Misha's base. And that might lead to being taken along by him on a mission. But when he'd worked up enough courage to ask one of the mechanics if he could help out, the man looked him over and said, "How old are you, son?"

"Going on thirteen," he replied.

"I'm afraid you're a little young for this kind of work," the man told him. "Besides, only Commander Zissman can assign anyone to a job. Talk to him and hear what he says."

Yes. He would talk to him. That is, if he were still here when the commander got back. In the meantime, when Chanele was in the kitchen or on lookout duty he would while away the time by wandering around the camp, which appeared to him like a small town in the middle of the forest. A town where all the inhabitants were Jews, and all busy working at something. He was the only idle one and it made him uncomfortable.

From time to time someone would stop him and say, "A newcomer?"

"Yes."

"From what ghetto?"

A familiar question. Every partisan at Uncle Misha's base had asked him that. And his answer always evoked a look of wonderment. A Jew who had succeeded in eluding the ghetto!

One afternoon he wandered farther into the forest than on previous walks and came upon something he didn't know existed in the camp—a tannery! Jews, bearded and unbearded, wearing leather aprons and high boots, their shirtsleeves rolled up, their faces beaded with perspiration, were standing over steaming kettles and stirring boiling hides with long sticks. Over them swirled a cloud of acrid vapors that wafted out into the forest, spreading the offensive odor beyond the tannery.

While some men were working at the kettles others were stretching the processed hides taut and hanging them on heavy ropes strung around tree trunks. Nobody took notice of him as he stood there, almost transfixed by the sight of a tannery in the forest. But just when he was ready to move on, a head bobbed up from under a cloud of steam at the far end of a row of kettles and it seemed to him a familiar face. Reb Pinches! His *melamed*! The itinerant Hebrew teacher who used to come to his house once a week to teach him Hebrew and the weekly portion of *Chumesh*, the Five Books of Moses. Was it possible? Was it really Reb Pinches, or was he imagining things? He focused hard on the figure but the steam kept obscuring his view. "Reb Pinches!" he finally called out.

The man stopped his stirring and looked up, his eyes piercing the dense vapors, staring at the caller. From a distance it was only a boy he saw, and as a melamed he knew many boys. Who was this one? He walked away from the kettle and as he approached the caller a smile appeared on his face.

"Motele! As true as I live, Leibel the miller's son!" He held out his wet hand, "*Sholem Aleichem*, Motele." They stood there, looking at each other in silence, as if their mutual discovery had rendered them speechless.

How his former teacher had changed! Motele thought. Reb Pinches's grimy, sweaty face looked tanned and leathery, as though it were fashioned from one of the hides hanging on the ropes. His eyes dull and bloodshot. His long, flowing beard shrunken and matted from the steam. Only his earlocks and skullcap reminded him of the old Reb Pinches.

"Yes," Reb Pinches sighed, as though sensing the boy's bewilderment. "Your melamed has turned into a tanner. Would you have believed it?" He paused, nodding thoughtfully. "But thank God one lives," he continued with a sigh. "Every living Jew these days is a miracle. You, I, and all of them here," he indicated the other tanners with a sweep of his hand, "miracles." He looked deep into the boy's face. "And you, Motele," he said, "are truly a miracle. I thought I had lost all my pupils. And here you are. How did you escape the German Angel of Death?"

"I was not at home. I was in town for my music lesson when they killed them." And as an afterthought he added. "My violin saved me."

"Not your violin, Motele. The One Above saved you. We have a great Father in heaven."

Great Father indeed! Motele thought bitterly. Why had the great Father chosen to spare only him? Was he more worthy of life than his parents and his sister Basha? No, if the One Above had it in His power to save him and He didn't save the others he had no thanks for the One Above. There were times when he felt so alone in the world he wished he had been home that day and shared his family's fate. He would have liked to tell this to Reb Pinches but he remembered that a pupil never questioned nor contradicted his melamed, so he said instead, "And you, Reb Pinches, did you escape from the ghetto?" Everyone he met so far had escaped from a ghetto.

"No," Reb Pinches said, "that's one pleasure I denied the Germans, shutting me up in a ghetto. So how do I come to the forest, you want to know? That's another miracle from the One Above," he raised his eyes heavenward. "I was on the way to a village to one of my pupils when suddenly I hear singing. I look up and I see Germans marching toward me. A swarm of Germans from nowhere. Like locusts descending on a field. I had enough presence of mind to run into a barn, and that saved my life.

"The peasant was a decent fellow and didn't turn me out. He sheltered me and fed me for several days. One day he came into the barn and told me that the Germans had shot all the Jewish families in the nearby villages, including Stare-Mloda, and that it was dangerous for him to hide me any longer. That day, when it grew dark, he gave me a loaf of bread, some boiled potatoes, and some apples and took me to the forest. And that's how I became a forest dweller.

"At night the wolves were roaming the forest. By day the Germans were roaming the countryside. And I was in the middle, afraid to move. One day that Good Angel, the peasant, came to warn me that I was still in danger. He told me the forester was boasting to everybody that he had discovered several Jews in the forest and pointed them out to the Germans. He advised me to go deeper into the forest, far away from the village. Now I was completely cut off from the world.

"One day I came eye-to-eye with a wolf. 'This is the end,' I thought, and started to mumble my confession. The wolf stood there looking at me, as though he were listening to the words. Then he turned and walked away. From that day on I stopped being afraid of the wolves in the forest, only of the wolves outside the forest.

"After a few days I came upon other Jews who were wandering around the forest without a morsel of food and without a destination. Were it not for Commander Zissman we would probably have disappeared without a trace. He gathered us together and brought us here. The younger ones became partisans who avenge the suffering of our people. And Jews like me do whatever we can to help the partisans. Who would have thought that Pinches melamed would ever become a tanner? And in a forest yet! But here I am, and thank God for that. . . . And you, Motele, how did you get here?"

"I came here to get well," he said. "I'm with Uncle Misha's partisans," Motele added self-consciously. He hoped he still was. He was not so certain anymore.

"Well," Reb Pinches held out his hand to say goodbye, "wherever you are may the One Above protect you from all evil."

Later Chanele explained to him why the camp needed its own tannery. Jews who escaped from the ghetto were in tatters; many of them barefoot. Partisans couldn't go out on missions without boots, and the camp population couldn't live through a winter barefoot. From peasants the partisans were allowed to take only food. Not clothing. This was a very strict rule. A partisan who broke it was severely punished. Now the camp was able to produce its own leather and make sheepskin coats and boots, first for the partisans and then for the rest of the camp dwellers. "We all earn our stay here by working for the partisans," she continued. "We do things for them they cannot do themselves, and they in turn provide us with food and protection. Without the partisan detachments in this area we'd either starve to death or be wiped out by Bandarov's bands of Ukrainian fascists who work hand in hand with the Germans."

"Have they attacked the camp?" Motele asked.

"More than once. But they were beaten back by our own and the other partisans. Now they don't come around anymore."

"If they ever come around again I'll get a hold of a Vyntovka and be out there with the partisans. I know how to handle one."

"You'll do whatever Commander Zissman tells you to," she said, "not what you want to do."

Motele made no reply. He knew she was right. A partisan acts on his commander's orders.

They had *their* tree where they met and from there they would go off to some quiet spot in the forest where they talked and sang. Chanele knew all the good walking paths and how far one could go without getting lost. That's what he and Basha used to do in Stare-Mloda, sneak off to the forest from time to time, and talk and sing duets to their hearts' content without calling attention to themselves.

Once he forgot himself and called her Basha. "I'm Chanele," she reminded him quietly. Then, seeing the sad look that came over his face, she said, "That's all right. I understand. Sometimes I have to remember not to call you Yankele. When you sing you remind so much of my brother. He had a lovely voice."

"Did you sing duets with him?"

"In the ghetto I did. In the courtyards."

"Children begged?"

"They had to beg or starve."

"What did you get for your singing?"

"Oh, they'd throw down a crust of bread, or a boiled potato, or a few pennies. Mostly pennies though, because they had no food themselves. The best begging was outside the ghetto."

"Were you allowed out?"

She gave him a look of surprise. Didn't he know that the ghetto was a prison and that the penalty for leaving it was death? Then she remembered that he had not been in a ghetto. "No," she said, "it was strictly forbidden. But the hunger was so great it didn't stop the young beggars. They'd crawl through a narrow opening in the ghetto wall, or climb over it and run before the guards spotted them. Sometimes they didn't make it. If they were lucky they'd come home with pocketsful of food. But getting back in was just as dangerous as getting out. One could get shot for smuggling food into the ghetto. That's how we lost my brother, Yankele." She fell silent and her face clouded with sadness.

He wished he could say something consoling but he didn't know what, and so they walked on in silence. He reached out for her hand and took it in his. Now the silence became more bearable for both of them.

The first song Chanele taught him was the "Partisan

Song." The author was Hirsh Glick, a young poet in the Vilno ghetto. A young woman who has escaped from that ghetto and, after much wandering, had found her way to this camp, brought it with her. She had sung it at a campfire and it became a favorite overnight. Now every young person in camp knew the "Partisan Song." Patiently Chanele sang it for him over and over again while he "took it down" on his violin:

'Twas a silent, starry night
And the frost was sharp and biting
Do you remember how I taught you
To hold a pistol in your hand?

A girl, a jacket, a beret
A pistol firmly in her hand
A girl with a velvet face
Struck the enemy caravan

She aimed her tiny pistol
She aimed, she shot, she hit
And with a single bullet
Stopped an autoful of arms.

At dawn she slipped out of the forest
A garland of snow in her hair
The victory was small, but oh, how sweet!
A victory for the Freedom Day.

Overnight Motele became a favorite of the young people in camp when he accompanied them on the violin as they sang the "Partisan Song."

As soon as it became known in camp that Commander Zissman was back, Motele, hair combed, coat buttoned, boots cleaned, appeared in his tent. The commander, a hulk of a man, almost twice the size of Uncle Misha, Motele thought, smiled at him warmly as he looked him over. "Well, you seem to be in much better shape than when they brought you here," the commander said. "How do you feel?"

"I feel fine."

"I have something for you that'll make you feel even better. I brought you regards from a very good friend of yours. Would you know who that is?"

"Yoshke?" Motele said after a pause.

"That's right. I saw him only yesterday."

"At Uncle Misha's base?"

"In Klynov. On the way back from our mission we stopped in Klynov for a little meeting with Uncle Misha and a few of his partisans. Yoshke was there too. 'Take good care of my friend, Motele,' he said to me, 'and tell him that the first chance I get I'll come to visit him.' "

"Just to visit me?" he said, looking at the commander, as though to make sure he'd heard him right. "He didn't say he would come for me?"

"Why, are you unhappy here?"

He was and he wasn't. He was certainly happy whenever he was with Chanele. And he looked forward to the walks, and the singing. And he enjoyed playing at the campfires. But all this, he'd thought, was temporary, a pleasant way of passing the time while he waited for Yoshke to come for him. "I want to be a partisan," he said.

"As soon as we find something for you to do you'll be a partisan."

"I mean a partisan who goes on missions."

"We can't *all* go on missions," the commander told him. "We don't have enough weapons even for those who are fit for combat. But when we help the frontline partisans we become behind-the-lines partisans. In that way we are *all* partisans, and that goes for you too." He paused, raising his finger and cocking his head to one side. "Listen." They stood there listening to the intermittent clanging that resounded through the forest. "That's Feivel shaping a horseshoe," the commander continued. "His hammering is a familiar sound here. It's the forest's heartbeat. All day long he shoes partisans' horses. And you know how important a horse is to a partisan going out on a mission. That's why Feivel, in his way, is also a partisan. You understand what I'm saying, Motele?"

"Yes," he nodded.

"Now tell me what you would like to do."

"I would like to work in the repair shop with Shloime."

"How old are you, Motele?"

"I'm going on thirteen."

"That means you're twelve. You're a little too young for the repair shop. It's heavy work. And dangerous too. What was your job in Uncle Misha's camp?"

"I had two jobs. I worked in the supply tent and I took care of the horses."

"You know your way around horses?"

"Yes. I was raised in a village. We had two horses. I can ride a horse real fast," he said eagerly, hoping it might lead to a mission.

"Then I'll talk to Feivel. He needs a helper. He's very fussy. So far none of the boys I sent him suited him. They were all city boys, afraid of horses, he told me. But you say you were raised in a village and know your way around horses."

"Yes," Motele said without enthusiasm.

"Well, maybe you'll have more luck with Feivel than the others did."

When Motele reported for work the next morning Feivel was already in the smithy, reviving the fire, breathing life into the smoldering coals with his makeshift bellows. For a while he took no notice of Motele, standing diffidently at his side. When he finally acknowledged the presence of his new apprentice it could hardly be called a welcome. "You're the fiddler, aren't you?" Feivel said gruffly. "Why, in God's name, a fiddler should want to be a blacksmith I don't know. Before the day is over you'll have callouses large as lima beans. A fiddle doesn't like a calloused hand."

How did he know what a fiddle liked or didn't like? Motele felt like asking. Did he ever play one? But something told him it would be smarter to keep his silence. In appearance Feivel reminded him somewhat of Yoshke. The short heavy-set figure; the beard covering most of his face; the quick jerky movements of the body. As for friendliness, he was no Yoshke.

When Feivel finally turned and looked at him he said, "I took you on only because the commander insisted. He told me you're not afraid of horses. All right, we'll see. All the other boys he sent me would tremble when a horse just swished his tail. Now go over to the clearing where the horses are tied up, untie one and bring it over. They're all going out on missions tonight and we have to see which of them needs shoeing."

Motele surveyed a dozen or so horses in the clearing and picked a large brown mare, only because she looked like the kind of horse anyone afraid of horses would not dare approach. As he reached for the reins the mare shook her mane, as if saying, "No! Don't touch!" And Motele patted her neck for a while before reaching for the reins again. Then he patted her belly and finally her nose, talking to the mare as though she were human,

"Now you be good. You hear me? You want me to lose my job on account of you?" The mare scratched the ground with her hind legs, as though threatening to rear up. "Now stand still, will you!" Motele commanded. "What kind of a partisan's horse are you, anyway?" He'd always talked to his own horses and it had worked. It worked now too. The mare let him untie her and then followed him docilely to the smithy. "Here she is," he announced to Feivel.

"At least you know it's a she," Feivel said. "The others couldn't even tell the difference between a he and a she." He took the reins from Motele and wound them around a stump. "Now lift up one of her hind legs. Let's see if she needs shoeing."

This was the moment Motele feared. Even friendly horses would sometimes balk at having their legs lifted by a stranger. But he remembered what the blacksmith in Klynov did when he brought a horse in for shoeing. He'd pat his flank a few times before touching the leg. Motele did the same thing and the mare gave him no trouble.

"She does need shoeing," Feivel pronounced, then went into the tent and returned with a leather apron. "Put this on," he said. "It'll save your pants." When Motele had the apron on Feivel studied him a moment and smiled at him for the first time, saying, "Now you look like a blacksmith's apprentice." Motele knew then he had the job.

At the end of the day he sought out Chanele and told

her of his triumph. Fussy Feivel had accepted him as his helper.

"Let's see your hands," she said.

He held out his hands palms up. His callouses were not as large as lima beans but they were almost the size of peas.

"I'll make you a pair of leather gloves," Chanele volunteered. "There are plenty of leather scraps outside the tannery. Surele will work on one and I on the other so it'll go faster."

"Feivel will laugh at me," he objected.

"So he'll laugh. It's more important that you think of your hands. You're a violinist."

"I'm a blacksmith now," he said, somewhat defiantly. "At least I'm learning to be one."

"But after the war you'll be a violinist again, so you have to protect your hands."

After the war. . . . He hadn't thought about after the war. And maybe he didn't want to think about it. After the war Jews in hiding will come out of their hiding places; partisans will come out of the forests, and they will go home. Where will *he* go? Back to Stare-Mloda? To whom? He once had relatives in Vilno. The closest was Uncle Boruch, his father's brother.

One day, when Motele was nine, a letter had come from Uncle Boruch, inviting them to his daughter's wedding. The journey to Vilno was a very long one but every moment of it was exciting. It was the first time he and Basha had ever been on a train; the first time they had seen a city as big as Vilno. And the wedding! For months afterwards that's all they talked about at home, the relatives and the wedding.

Later, when the Nazis killed his family and he wandered from village to village, sleeping in barns and in fields, he clung to the memory of that wedding and the relatives he'd met in Vilno for the first and only time. He felt close to all of them, even the distant ones. They were all he now had in the world.

And then he lost them too. He had learned from a new partisan in Uncle Misha's detachment, who had escaped from the Vilno ghetto, that Uncle Boruch and his family were killed by the Germans. The man had mentioned the dread word, Ponary, a wooded place about fifteen kilometers from Vilno, which became a mass grave of the Vilno Jews.

"I don't even know where I'll be after the war," he said to Chanele, "so why should I worry about it now?"

"If you want to you could come with us. Surele and I already talked about it. We talk a lot about what we'll do after the war. First we'll go back to our home town, and whoever is now living in our house will have to give it back to us. Everybody in the town knows it's ours. And now that we're just the two of us there'll be plenty of room for you. You can have a room all to yourself. And as soon as we get settled we'll start searching for relatives."

"I don't have any relatives to search for anymore."

"How do you know? Maybe some of them were lucky and are in hiding someplace, like my uncle and aunt. Miracles can happen, you know."

"That's what Reb Pinches said. Every one of us here is a miracle."

"Then will you come to live with us?"

He thought a moment and, looking gratefully at Chanele, said, "I can earn my keep by playing at weddings."

"Come," she said, taking his hand.

"Where to?"

"To the tannery. To look for some scraps of leather before it gets dark."

9 Late one afternoon Commander Zissman sent word to Motele to report to him after work. For the rest of the day Motele could think of nothing else but that message. He hoped it would have something to do with a mission. But that didn't seem very likely. He hadn't been near a Vyntovka, or any other kind of weapon ever since he left Uncle Misha's base, which was nearly three months ago.

Feivel too was brooding over the message. At one point, as they were shoeing a horse, he muttered, as though to himself: "If he thinks he's going to take you away from here he'll have to reckon with me." Coming from Feivel, who was not one to hand out compliments, this was indeed high praise. If it's just being switched to another job, Motele thought, he too wouldn't want it to happen. He liked what he was doing. Shoeing partisans' horses was almost like oiling their weapons. It was the closest a behind-the-line's partisan could come to going on a mission.

Later, on the way to the commander's tent, a thought

occurred to him. What if he found Yoshke there, waiting to take him back to Uncle Misha's base? Would he really want to go back now? He thought of Chanele and Surele, with whom he had made a pact to live with after the war, and whom he would miss very much if he had to leave now. He thought of the campfires, the singing, the playing, the many friends he had made, and he was torn because he knew that one thing he would not refuse was going on a mission. And if that was why Yoshke had come for him he would go. It was with these thoughts that Motele entered the commander's tent.

The commander came to the point at once. "I'll tell you why I sent for you, Motele. I have a favor to ask of you. You know our cook, Braindel, don't you?"

"Yes."

"She's a widow. Her entire family perished. The pits . . . . Somehow she managed to survive. One of those miracles. And Ephraim, who works in the tailor shop, you know, don't you?"

"Yes."

"He too lost his entire family. Well, this morning they came to me with the news that they want to get married. Right here in camp. Naturally, I gave my permission and wished them *mazeltov*. This will be the first wedding in our family camp, and I would like you to play at the wedding. Will you do it?"

"Yes."

"Fine. I'm glad to hear it. You have two weeks to prepare. And now that that's settled, how's your work at the smithy?"

"It's all right. I like the job."

"I know that Feivel is pleased with you. And he's a hard man to please. So you must be doing all right." When the commander shook hands with him before he left the tent he thanked him again for agreeing to play at the wedding.

It was a cool but bright October day. Shortly before noon the bell rang and all the camp dwellers dropped their work and began to gather at the "Square," a large clearing in the forest where partisans assembled before going out on a mission, or coming back from one. It was also the place where the commander addressed them from time to time, bringing them news on the progress of the war, reporting on missions both successful and otherwise, and taking up special problems of work and discipline. But on this day the Square took on a festive air it had not known before.

Strung across two trees was a large strip of white cloth bearing these words in hand-printed Hebrew: MAZEL-TOV EPHRAIM AND BRAINDEL. In the center of the Square stood a makeshift canopy consisting of four poles and a blanket on top. Surrounding it, in horse-shoe shape, were several long makeshift tables laden with food. Very few in the crowd had on what might be called holiday clothes. In the forest the quality of

a garment was judged by the amount of patches it had.
The fewer the patches the higher the quality. Still, many
managed in one way or another to enhance their appearance for this special occasion. Women washed their hair.
Men scrubbed the mud off their boots. And those who
had a piece of jewelry displayed it proudly. Chanele
wove a red ribbon into her braids and wore a flower-
print kerchief around her neck. She stayed close to Motele, holding his violin case for him while he, more
from nervousness than necessity, kept tuning up his instrument. Feivel, the blacksmith, came without his
leather apron, and that was his concession to dressing
up for the wedding.

Promptly at noon the wedding began. Reb Pinches,
his beard combed and wearing his black caftan, con-
ducted the first part of the ceremony in Hebrew. After
the groom had stepped on the glass and kissed the bride
the melamed made a brief speech in Yiddish. "Our sages
had something to say about marriage," he began. "It
is written in the Gemara that Rabbi Johanan said: 'If
a man's first wife dies it is as if the Temple were de-
stroyed in his day.' And Rabbi Alexandri said: 'If a
man's wife dies the world becomes dark for him.' Why
do I speak of this on a day of rejoicing? Because our
joys are mingled with sorrow, and the mouth must not
deny the voice of the heart. When the heart cries out
in pain the mouth must give it voice.

"I look about me and wherever I see a man I see a

darkened world. Our sages spoke of the death of a wife. Is not the same true of the death of a husband?" A wail went up from the crowd. Women cried openly, and men wiped tears from their eyes. "We are a people of faith," Reb Pinches continued. "This wedding under the open sky in a forest is yet another example of the boundless faith of our people. Snatched from the hands of the Angel of Death we celebrate life. So let me conclude with the words of another great rabbi, Rabbi Akiba, who said: 'He is wealthy who possesses a virtuous wife.' You, Ephraim, are now such a wealthy man. We all rejoice in your wealth. Mazeltov!"

"Mazeltov! Mazeltov!" the words rang out in the forest, and at that moment at least the joy overwhelmed the sorrow.

Someone tapped Motele on the shoulder. It was Commander Zissman. "Now musician," he said, "play something lively, something fitting for a wedding," and he lifted him up onto the bench. It all happened so quickly and unexpectedly it stunned him. From where he stood the crowd looked tremendous. He had never seen so many people close together. He was so nervous the palms of his hands grew moist.

Earlier in the day he had gone through with Chanele his entire repertoire of Yiddish songs she had taught him and it was her idea that he begin with a love lyric called, "*Reyzele*," and conclude with the "Partisan Song." But at this moment his mind seemed to have gone blank. Although he'd tuned the instrument a while ago he began tuning it again to gain some time to collect his thoughts. *"Nu, Klezmer,* play, play," he heard the commander's impatient voice. He stuck the violin under his chin and instead of *"Reyzele"* he struck up a song from his old repertoire of two, *"Lomir Zich Iberbeten"* ("Let's Make Up"). It was greeted with a burst of laughter.

What had he done? he wondered. Was there something about his playing, or his appearance that brought on this laughter? He didn't know *"Lomir Zich Iberbeten"* was a funny song. By the time he got to the second verse they were not only laughing, they were singing too. They all seemed to know it and each new verse brought a fresh burst of laughter. He caught a glimpse of the commander and when he saw him singing and laughing with the others he decided he had made the right choice of song and played with gusto.

From then on the crowd sang to every song he played. It was as though he were conducting a mass chorus with his violin. And the gay mood inspired by the first song prevailed throughout. But when he began to play *"Partizaner Lied"* there was an instant change of mood. Gaiety gave way to seriousness. The voices were solemn, the faces resolute. It was as though they were singing a vow. And then Commander Zissman mounted the tree stump from which he always addressed a crowd.

"My fellow partisans," he began, smiling, his eyes coming to rest on Motele. "To the best of my knowledge our musician is still a bachelor, but he already seems to know something about the life of married couples. They quarrel, they make up. Maybe that's why he chose as his first song, '*Lomir Zich Iberbeten.*' " There was laughter again and now Motele understood why they had laughed before.

The commander waited for the laughter to subside; then he continued: "I also remember another time and another kind of laughter connected with this song and I think that today, on this festive occasion of a Jewish wedding in the forest, is the proper time to recall it.

"This goes back to the days before the ghetto, the first days of the occupation when the Germans celebrated their entrance into a town by staging a pogrom on Jews. But they were not satisfied with just shooting and looting. Their victims had to amuse them as well. In my own town they rounded up all the Jews they could find— men, women, children—and marched us to the square. There they ordered us to sing and dance. The graves of our beloved were still fresh and they wanted us to sing and dance. 'Louder! Faster!' they shouted, prodding us with their rifle butts and bayonet points.

"So we sang louder and moved faster, bumping into each other, falling over each other, and the more confusing the scene looked and the more comical it appeared, the more the Germans liked it. And all the while their film cameras were grinding away and their sound tracks picking up our voices. This was a spectacle with a double purpose: amusement for themselves and a propaganda film for Germany. They wanted to show the Germans back home how depraved and debased were the Jews. In the middle of a war, their homeland invaded and occupied, the Jews have nothing better to do than to sing and dance. An utterly irresponsible and self-indulgent people.

"We had to sing only Yiddish songs and none other. Somebody remembered '*Zomir Zich Iberbeten*,' a song most of us knew. The tune seemed to appeal to the Germans. '*Noch einmal!*' they shouted when we finished. So we sang it again. But that was not the end of it. Over and over again they made us sing that same song. We were weary. We were falling off our feet. Our throats were dry and our eyes were moist. But we had to go on singing '*Lomir Zich Iberbeten*.'

"Suddenly something unexpected happened. A young woman who was right behind me decided to change one phrase of the song, the most oft-repeated phrase. Whenever she came to the words '*lomir zich iberbeten*,' * she sang instead, '*mir velen zei iberleben*.'**

"At first we were confused. Some picked up the phrase and some didn't. But by the time we got to the third stanza we all sang out the words, as though with one throat, and with such force and conviction that the air around us vibrated. And the Germans didn't have to order us to repeat that song. If we had to sing that was the song we wanted to sing. 'That's more like it,' the

* Let's make up
** We shall overcome

Germans said, 'Now you're singing and not wailing.' Their camera man moved in closer to catch the expressions on our faces, and the sound-track man called out, 'Louder, louder!' and we obliged.

"That was our first lesson in resistance. Right now, at this very moment, the words *'mir velen zei iberleben,'* are probably ringing out in some movie theater in Germany. Most of the Jews who sang those words have already perished. But we here, and all the other Jewish partisans in the forests of Poland, Volhenia, Lithuania, and Byelorussia are making good their vow, singing a new song *'Partizaner Lied,'* and singing it not only with words but with hand grenades and Vyntovkas, with everything that destroys the enemy.

"The other day I caught on our shortwave radio one of the harangues Hitler delivered in Breslau. He assured his mob that if one Jew will still be alive after the war he, personally, will make him a minister. Our answer to him is, 'Thanks for the honor.' After the war we Jews will appoint our own minister, and more than one. But first we will dance on Hitler's grave.

"I think a fitting way to conclude this celebration is to sing once again, *'Lomir Zich Iberbeten,'* only this time we'll sing the words the way the Jews of my home town sang it that day of the Square—*'mir velen zei iberleben.'* That's our answer to Hitler's fantasies." He turned to look for Motele and when he found him called out, "Musician, lead off!"

Motele leaped on the bench and began to play. At

that moment his violin was a Vyntovka and he was under his commander's orders. He moved his bow boldly
and vigorously, straining the strings to the utmost. And
when he came to the phrase, *"lomir zich iberbeten"* he
swung his head upward as he bore down with his bow,
and a chorus of sixteen hundred voices thundered, *"mir
velen zei iberleben! iberleben!"* Never before had he
put so much feeling into a song. And when he'd finished
the violin trembled in his hand. All of him trembled.
Applause mingled with shouts of, "More! More!" He
saw the commander himself applauding. Should he play
the song over again, or take a bow and step down? He
was confused. The whole camp wanted him to do something and he didn't know exactly what. He felt someone tugging at his coat. It was Chanele, " *'Partizaner
Lied,'* " she called up to him. He stuck the violin under
his chin and closed his eyes. This was a lyrical song, calling for a slower tempo. The voices rose and fell with
the movements of his bow, while the forest stood in silence, as though listening. They were still applauding
when he jumped off the bench.

"You were wonderful," Chanele said, looking long
and admiringly into his eyes and, leaning forward,
kissed him. He blushed and she made believe she didn't
notice. "You're perspiring," she said, wiping his blushing face with the palm of her hand.

10 One morning when Motele came to the clearing to see which of the horses needed shoeing he saw one standing apart from the others, its head deep in a bag of oats that hung from its neck. He recognized it at once as Yoshke's spotted mare. To make certain he was not mistaken he pulled the bag away and there was the familiar white spot on the mare's face. "Where's Yoshke?" he demanded, as though expecting the horse to tell him. The way the mare stared at him and swished her tail he knew she recognized his voice. His heart was beating fiercely. Yoshke was here, somewhere! But where? He started to run and stopped. Which way? The commander's tent. If Yoshke is here on partisan business that's where he would be, with the commander. But the commander's tent was quite a distance from here, and he had Feivel to reckon with. He changed his mind. He would run back to the smithy and tell Feivel that he must go look for Yoshke. He would not work until he found him.

As he was approaching the smithy Motele recognized

Yoshke from a distance. He ran straight up to him and the two held each other in a long embrace. He knew he should say something but he was too overwhelmed for words. Right now the security of Yoshke's arms around him was all that mattered.

It was Yoshke who broke the silence: "I got a good report about you from Commander Zissman," he said. "He's very pleased with you. And so is your boss here. Am I right, Reb Feivel?"

"What's true is true," Feivel said. "For a fiddler he's not a bad apprentice. At least he can tell the difference between a horse's mane and his tail."

Yoshke's large frame shook with laughter.

"Will you be here long?" Motele spoke up.

Yoshke shook his head. "We have to be on our way soon."

Motele wondered who else was here from Uncle Misha's detachment and whether Feivel would give him a few minutes off to talk to Yoshke. "Is Luba here?" he asked.

"I'm here alone. I came especially for you."

"For me?" Motele asked, as though he wasn't sure he had heard him right.

"For whom else?" Yoshke said. "Of course for you."

Motele was torn. He wanted so to be with Yoshke; and he couldn't bear the thought of being separated from Chanele. He knew he would miss her terribly. Surele too, but especially Chanele. And he would even miss his work at the smithy. Compared to sorting uniforms in Avremel's supply tent, or cleaning weapons which he himself never got to use, shoeing partisans' horses was exciting.

"Nu, fiddler," Feivel said, "why do you stand there like a clay *golem*? Take off your apron. Unless you want to show your friend how you shoe a horse."

"I'm afraid we don't have time for that," Yoshke said. "Your apprentice is needed for a very special mission. That's why I started out at dawn to arrive here early."

A special mission! That meant he could come back afterwards. But he must run to the kitchen first. To tell Chanele where he was going. To assure her he would be back. He quickly removed the apron and handed it to Feivel. Then he turned to Yoshke. "Please wait for me here. I'll be back in a few minutes."

"Go get your things and don't be long. I'll be at the clearing where the horse is."

Motele shook hands with Feivel who said, "Go, and do a good job on whatever you have to do, and come back here. Nobody will take your place from you."

"I'll be back," Motele said, more for his own reassurance than for Feivel's, and he ran off. He didn't stop running until he reached the kitchen tent. Chanele was sitting with a group of girls, peeling potatoes. He caught her attention and she came out. "What happened?" she asked, seeing him panting for breath.

"Yoshke is here," he heaved out the words.

He had not mentioned Yoshke for some time and she had to think a moment to recall who he was.

"He came for me. I'm going on a mission—a special mission." He'd given her the most difficult part of the news and felt relieved until he saw tears gathering in her eyes.

"It's just for a while," he said, "I'll be back."

She looked at him, as though searching his face for assurance of his promise. "Did Yoshke tell you that?"

Motele shook his head.

"Then how do you know you'll be back?"

"Because I want to. And I want you to keep my violin while I'm gone."

"You won't need it?"

"What for? I'm going on a mission, not to play. A *special* mission, Yoshke said." He held out his hand.

"Aren't you going for the violin?"

"I haven't the time. Yoshke is waiting for me at the clearing. You can go over for it later."

"I'll take good care of it," she said, then she quickly brushed her lips against his and disappeared into the tent before he could see her cry.

As Yoshke was helping Motele up onto the horse he suddenly stopped and let him down on the ground. "Where's your fiddle?" he demanded. "You forgot your fiddle."

"I didn't forget it. I left it with a friend who'll take good care of it."

"Well, you better go get it because you'll need it."

"You said I was going on a special mission—"

"That's right. And the fiddle is part of it. Very much part of it."

"Will I have to play at a wedding?"

"What you'll have to do Uncle Misha himself will tell you. He's the commander and he gives the orders. All I can tell you is to hurry up and get the fiddle."

So it's the violin again and not the Vyntovka. Motele thought, as he ran to his tent. How can you fight the enemy with a violin? Special mission indeed! And what would he tell Chanele? Maybe he should tell her that he'd miss the violin; that he never traveled without it. No. He would tell her the truth.

To his surprise he found her sitting on the doorstep of his tent, holding the violin case on her lap, as though she had expected him back.

"I came for the violin," he said, unhappily.

"Why did you change your mind?"

"I didn't. Yoshke sent me for it. He says I'll need it for the special mission."

"I'm so glad," she said, smiling.

"I'm not."

"You should be. You're so lucky. Maybe you won't need a gun. You can be a partisan with your violin. You said it was a special mission, didn't you?"

"Yoshke said it."

"Maybe that's what makes it special. Your violin. You're probably the only one in the whole forest." She rose and handed him the instrument, adding, "I feel better now. I know how well you can handle this weapon."

Because of what she said he too felt better now. He walked her back to the kitchen tent. They shook hands again. Now it was he who kissed her, and quickly turned to go before she could see him blush.

11 That same day, in the afternoon, Motele was sitting face-to-face with Uncle Misha in the commander's tent. "Let me tell you why I sent for you," Uncle Misha said, leaning forward and taking a long pause before speaking again. "The day after tomorrow will be the beginning of an important Christian holiday. Peasants from all the nearby villages will come to the Greek Orthodox church in Ovrutch to attend services. The celebration will last a whole week.

"To get to Ovrutch one must cross a bridge, which is guarded day and night by German and Ukrainian police; and one must have a special permit from the local police. We found out from our contact that the Germans have suspended this rule for the duration of the holiday and everyone will be allowed to cross the bridge without a special permit.

"Naturally, we partisans want to take advantage of this. Ovrutch happens to be the seat of the German regional command. All the administrative offices are there. We want to know where they are located, how well they are guarded, and when the guard changes. For this reason I am sending into Ovrutch six partisans disguised as peasants, and I want you to go as one of the holiday beggars. The town will be swarming with them.

"Unload your entire repertoire of Russian and Ukrainian folk songs on Ovrutch. And begin with the church on the morning of the holiday. That's where all the beggars will be. If you're elsewhere that morning it'll look suspicious. After the services you mingle with the crowds in the square. But always as a beggar, and always keep your eyes and ears open for any scrap of information that might be of use to us.

"Don't talk to any of the partisans, and don't let on that you recognize any of them even if one happens to stand right near you. But if he approaches you and drops a coin in your cup it means he has a message for you to take to our contact, Keril. Yoshke will tell you where you'll find him."

"Is Yoshke one of the six?"

"Yes. And you'll meet the others before you go, so you can recognize them. And if you should see something happening to one of them—if he's being taken away by a .German or Ukrainian gendarme—report it immediately to Keril. Is all this clear to you?"

"Yes."

"One more thing and I'm through with the instructions," Uncle Misha said, reaching for a piece of paper on his desk. "I'm providing you with proper identification. We have a stamp-maker here who can make a forged document look more genuine than the real one." He unfolded the paper and studied it a moment. "Your first name is the only thing you'll recognize here," he said. "Yoshke told him your Ukrainian name was Mitek. The rest he made up himself. As of now you are Mitek Dubinov, son of Ivan Dubinov. You come from Listvin, a village in the region of Vlednik. What are you doing in Ovrutch? You're on the way to Zhitomir, looking for your father who, you think, is in one of the Russian prisoner-of-war camps. You've been on the road for a long time and you maintain yourself by begging and playing the violin." He handed Motele the document. "Study it and commit it to memory."

Uncle Misha rose, stepped away from the desk and surveyed the boy from head to toe. "I'm not so happy about your general appearance," he finally said. "You look a little too neatly dressed for a street beggar. You looked more the part when I first saw you. What did they do there at the camp, give you a new set of clothes?"

"Everything is the same. They just shortened the coat and sewed on some buttons so I don't have to hold it together with a rope. And they gave me another pair of boots."

"A rope. That's more likely. I'm afraid, Motele, we'll have to tear the buttons off your coat so you can tie a rope around it. As for the boots. . ." he examined them again, "just muddy them up a bit. Now come with me to the supply tent. Avremel will fit you out with a cup and whatever else you need to look like a beggar. Avremel is a very good make-up man."

The Greek Orthodox church of Ovrutch was a massive stone structure surrounded by a high wall. It towered over the town like some medieval fortress. All the beggars in the Ukraine seemed to have congregated in Ovrutch that morning. And they were all at the church. By the time Motele arrived there was not a single space left on either side of the front wall and he had to content himself with being the last in a long line of beggars. Some, he learned, had been there all night to assure for themselves the most desirable spot, the one closest to the entrance.

And the beggars were as varied in their beggarly appearance as they were numerous. By far the largest number were the war casualties, men with empty sleeves and empty trouser legs, folded and pinned to the upper parts to indicate the size of the missing limbs. There were blind old men led by wives or daughters; men and women with large tumors protruding from their heads and throats; men and women with ugly skin diseases on their faces and hands, all proclaiming their special deformities in the most plaintive of voices. Some sang sad Ukrainian songs and accompanied themselves on accordions; others stood motionless and silent, letting their disabilities plead for them.

As Motele was taking his violin out of the case he wondered how he could make himself heard in this wailing cacophony. But as he began to sing and play the popular Ukrainian folksong, "The Ant," the worshippers stopped to listen. Totally without any deformity, he had only his voice and violin to recommend him, and he scored with both. The onlookers showed particular interest in his playing. The bold, swift strokes of the bow and the nimble movements of his fingers on the strings drew melody from the instrument as though by magic. Clearly, here was not just another beggar who was playing, but a player who was begging.

The coins kept falling into the tin cup Avremel had scrounged up for him with ever greater frequency, and Motele kept nodding his thanks to the generous donators without interrupting his playing. Young peasant girls called out their favorites and Motele obliged. One girl was so taken with his performance that she put some potato pirogy into the linen sack that lay at his feet. The other beggars looked with envy and chagrin at this young upstart who stole the crowd's sympathy and attention away from them. And he wasn't even a cripple!

Suddenly Motele became aware of a commotion a short distance from where he was standing. The Ukrainian policeman who had been circulating in the crowd all morning to keep order was now pushing the people to either side to make room for an approaching German officer and his companion, a pretty military nurse. Motele went on playing as though nothing was happening. If he stopped playing, he thought, he might betray his fear that the German was coming for him. Sure enough the officer and the young lady stopped near him and didn't move. They just stood there, listening to his singing and playing. He kept his eyes on the violin. To look at them would make him more nervous than he already was.

A hush fell over the crowd. Everyone was now watching the Germans. Even the beggars ceased their wailing and craned their heads in his direction. *"Der kleine spielt ausgezeichnet,"* he heard the officer say to his companion.

"Er spielt wunderbar," the nurse replied.

From his knowledge of Yiddish Motele understood enough German to know they were praising his playing. He now dared look at them. Upon meeting his eyes the nurse smiled at him; the officer maintained his military reserve throughout. As soon as Motele had finished the number the officer touched his shoulder with his riding crop and said, *"Kom mit mir."*

Motele understood him but assumed a puzzled look. *"Kom, kom,"* the officer repeated, this time in a more commanding tone.

As he put the violin back in the case Motele thought: If only my hands were free I could make a dash for it and disappear in the crowd. With the violin in my hand that's impossible. A peasant woman who helped him tie the sack around his back whispered in Ukrainian, "Have no fear, have no fear."

It was not fear that he felt at that moment but shame. His first time out on a special mission, and caught! He wondered what happened to the others; had they too been betrayed or only he? Of one thing he was certain: No matter what the tortures he would not betray his comrades.

Once again the Ukrainian policeman cleared a path for them, running ahead all the way to the bottom of the winding slope where a military car was waiting. It was an open-top vehicle and this gave Motele the hope that when they rode through the square Yoshke, or any other of the partisans, would notice him and take whatever steps were necessary. He even imagined a daring prison rescue. He could see Avremel dressed as a German officer and armed with a forged document present himself at the prison to claim him. He would then be able to tell Chanele that the same partisan who saved her and Surele's life also saved his. It was a comforting thought.

The officer ordered him to get in front, next to the chauffeur, and to the chauffeur he said, "*Offizieren Haus.*" They drove in the opposite direction from town, and before Motele could figure out what the two words meant they had already turned into a broad semicircular driveway lined with limousines and other military vehicles. They drove up to a sprawling one-story structure over the entrance of which fluttered a black swastika flag. Below it a sign in large black letters read: *Deutsches Offizieren Haus*. The armed guard saluted and opened the door for them.

The first thing that caught Motele's eye when he entered the large, noisy, smoke-filled room on the first floor was a huge portrait of Hitler that hung from the wall opposite the door. It was a full-length figure of the Führer, his right arm thrust out, returning the Hitler salute. The walls were lined with small dining tables, which were crowded with German officers eating, drinking, and talking, while pretty Ukrainian waitresses were dashing about the room with trays laden with food and drinks.

The nurse stopped at one of the tables and never rejoined them. The officer took him to a corner of the room where an elderly gray-haired man in civilian clothes sat at a small, brown piano playing a medley that was lost in the din of talk and laughter. The man stopped playing and rose to his feet. The officer spoke to him in German and the pianist then turned to Motele and said, in Ukrainian, "Do you read notes?"

"Yes, sir."

"All right, let's see how well you play." He picked out a sheet of music from a heap on top of the piano and opened it. It was Paderewski's Minuet. Motele tuned up his instrument and, with the sack still on his

back, began to play to the man's accompaniment. At
the sound of the violin the noises began to subside and
diners turned their heads toward the corner where Motele stood. At the end of the playing there was a burst
of applause and shouts of "Bravo!"

"*Der kleine spielt gut,*" he heard the officer say to the
old man.

"*Sehr gut,*" the pianist replied.

The officer asked Motele to come with him to his of-
fice, and took the pianist along as interpreter. Once
again the first thing Motele saw upon entering the of-
fice was a portrait of Hitler. On this one the Führer
held his hands cockily on his chest and, instead of his
arm, his chin was thrust out. The officer sat down behind his desk. "Well, young fellow," he said to Motele,
"you're a lucky little devil. Your begging days are over.
You'll be a musician here in the German Officers House.
You'll play from twelve to two in the afternoon, and
from seven to eleven in the evening. For that you'll get
five German marks a week and your lunches and dinners
free. Well, how does that suit you?"

Motele hesitated. The thought of entertaining the
murderers of his parents and Basha, of Chanele's and
Surele's parents, of all the Jews that were dragged to the
pits, revolted him. He would sooner be in prison. There
he would at least be with those who worked against the
Nazis and not with those who worked with them, like
this old man, the pianist. "I have to find my father," he

said, thinking this to be the best excuse for not accepting the offer.

"Where is your father?" the officer wanted to know.

"In some prisoner-of-war camp in Zhitomir. I was on my way there but stopped to earn a little money playing."

"Do you know which camp in Zhitomir?"

"No. We heard a rumor that he was in one of the camps. That's all I know."

"If he's in one of the Zhitomir camps I am in a better position to locate him than you are. I'll write to the commandant of the region at once. What's your father's name?"

"Ivan Dubinov," Motele said, reaching for the document. The officer copied down the name and gave it back to him. "What does your father do?"

"Mechanic," the word popped into Motele's head.

"Auto mechanic?"

"Yes, sir."

"We can always use a good auto mechanic around here. If they locate your father I'll have him transferred to our motor pool in Ovrutch. How would that suit you?"

"Thank you, sir."

"As for lodging. Do you have a place to stay?"

"No, sir. I'm on the move all the time."

"I thought so," the officer said. He took out his wallet and assessed its contents. "Tell you what I'll do. I'll give you a week's salary in advance. Get yourself a room and a haircut. That leaves one more item to take care of, your clothes." He pushed a button on his desk and a guard appeared. "Send in my chauffeur," he told the guard. Presently the chauffeur arrived, saluted, and remained at attention. "Franz," the officer said, "right after lunch I want you to take this fellow to our tailor shop and have him measured for a soldier's uniform. Tell them I want it done as quickly as possible. In the meantime let them sew a few buttons on his coat so he can throw away that silly-looking rope."

"Yes, sir," the chauffeur clicked his heels and saluted again before he left.

Pointing to the pianist, the officer said to Motele, "From now on he will be your boss. You'll take orders from Herr Saldowski."

"Yes, sir."

Herr Saldowski, Motele surmised, was a Volksdeutscher, a German living in the Ukraine, and that was why he spoke German fluently and was addressed by a German as Herr. He warned himself to be on guard. Volksdeutscher were known for their collaboration with the Germans. He made up his mind that as soon as he got rid of the chauffeur he would report to Keril and leave town at once. Either Keril himself would take him to Klynov, or he would hitch a ride with some peasant. From Klynov he could easily make it back to the forest.

Before going back to the dining hall the pianist took

Motele to the kitchen, which was located in the back of the building on the ground floor, with a special stairway leading to the dining hall. "Barash," he said to the cook, a heavy-set Ukrainian of about fifty with one towel around his neck and another hanging from his shoulder, "this is my new assistant, Mitek. He'll play the violin. Give the boy something to eat because he'll soon have to work for two hours without a stop. And I better go up and have my own lunch."

The cook resented this sudden intrusion so close to lunchtime, and as soon as Herr Saldowski was gone he said to Motele, "Look here, fiddler, in the future you come down for your meal either before eleven, or after two."

In the future, thought Motele, you won't see me again. One of the Ukrainian kitchen girls cleared a space for him at the end of the kitchen counter and the other brought him his lunch—a plate of stuffed cabbage with boiled potatoes.

Promptly at two the chauffeur appeared in the doorway and motioned to Motele to come down. Motele picked up his sack and violin and was about to leave when the pianist said, "Leave the instrument here. It'll only be in your way."

"I don't mind."

"You may not mind but it's foolish to drag it along

a whole afternoon, first to the tailor, then hunting for a room. Use your head."

Reluctantly Motele put the violin back on the piano top.

"Make sure you are back here no later than five," the pianist told him. "I want to go over with you what we'll be playing tonight. And you need time for your supper."

"Yes, sir."

Some of the officers waved to him as he passed their tables on the way out. *"Sehr gut, sehr gut,"* they said. At any other place he would have acknowledged the compliments with a smile and a nod of the head. Here he blushed with shame at having entertained them. He passed them by quickly, eager to be on the other side of the door.

The tailors kept him for over an hour, measuring him for a new uniform and looking for matching buttons for his coat. When he came out of the shop it was already past three. He still had to get a haircut, find lodging, report to Keril, and be back at the Officers House by five. He ran to Keril first.

Keril, a much younger man than any of the six partisans with whom he had come into town this morning, greeted him with a big smile and a vigorous handshake, saying, "You're certainly a fast worker, Mitek. First day in town and you land yourself a good job."

Motele was puzzled by Keril's greeting. Was he teasing him for his failure the first day on the mission? Was he glad to see him free? He didn't know.

"You do have the job, I hope," Keril said, fixing a serious look on Motele's face.

"Yes. How do you know?"

"Captain Schultzberger would take you to only one place: the German Officers House. He's in charge there. Around eleven in the morning he usually picks up his girl friend at the hospital and takes her to lunch. Fortunately he stopped off at the church to see what was happening and liked your playing. By the way, I liked it too."

"You were there?"

Keril nodded.

"I didn't see you."

"That's good. You were not supposed to see me."

After a thoughtful pause Motele said, "I won't work there. I'll play tonight to get my violin back. Then I'll run away."

"You're not running anywhere," Keril said, firmly. "You just stay where you are."

"I will not work for the enemy. They killed my parents and my sister."

"And they killed my younger brother, who was a partisan, and they dragged my only sister off to Germany for slave labor and I haven't heard from her in a year. Still, I would grab the chance to work in the German

Officers House even if it was to clean toilets. Don't you see, Mitek, we desperately need a pair of eyes and ears there and you say you want to run away."

"What will I have to do there?"

"I have a pretty good idea. But the instructions must come from Uncle Misha himself. I'm making a special trip to Klynov tonight to tell him about your job. You be back here tomorrow morning and I'll tell you what your assignment is. In the meantime, congratulations. I can just see Uncle Misha's face when he hears about your job. He'll be very pleased."

12 "First I should tell you that Uncle Misha was delighted to hear about your job," Keril said to Motele the next morning. "He regards it as the most important thing to come out of this special mission. As for your assignment: You are to study the insignias and unit numbers on the officers' uniforms, as well as their rank. And you should eavesdrop on their conversations. How's your German?"

"Some words I can understand. If they sound like Yiddish."

"Good. Mark them down."

"How will I know they're important?"

"That's not your worry. Moscow will decide whether they're important or not."

"Moscow?"

"Every scrap of information you'll pick up will be sent to Partisan Headquarters in Moscow. Ovrutch is an important railway junction. German troop trains heading east stop here for transfer, and before fanning out to the various sections of the eastern front the officers are wined and dined at the German Officers House. In Moscow they're very eager to know what units are going where. And you are in that strategic position to gather this vital information. Now you know why you must do your best to hold on to that job."

Motele was silent, overwhelmed by the awesome responsibility placed on him. He suddenly remembered Chanele's parting words to him: "You're so lucky. You can be a partisan with your violin. You're probably the only one in the whole forest. . . ." He hadn't fully understood her then. Now he did. "Yes," he nodded. "I know."

From that day on he met with Keril every afternoon between three and four o'clock to report what he had seen and heard the night before and at lunch time. Twice that first week Keril praised him for his eye for detail and his good memory. And at the end of the week he brought praise from Uncle Misha himself.

And the pianist, Herr Saldowski, was so pleased with his playing that he took a fatherly interest in him. Was he satisfied with his lodgings? Did he have enough pocket money? Did Barash, the cook, feed him well? If not he would talk to him. One day when he returned from lunch the pianist invited him to his table and said, "I have a feeling that in a few weeks from now you won't have to eat in the kitchen anymore. As soon as you get your new uniform I will look for the opportunity to talk to Captain Schultzenberger about it. As a rule they don't allow Slavs to eat in the same room with

Germans. But they might make an exception in your case, especially with your German uniform on. By the way, when will it be ready?"

"I don't know," Motele said. "I had my second fitting yesterday."

"Ukrainian tailors," the old man shook his head contemptuously, "what do you expect? If German tailors ran this shop your uniform would have been ready a long time ago." In a lowered voice he added, "And they steal right and left. Material disappears and turns up on the black market. It's plain sabotage, no doubt about it. If you don't get your uniform soon I'll talk to the captain. Don't you worry."

"Thank you, sir," Motele said, trying to sound appreciative. Although he knew it was inevitable he tried not to think about it. The thought of having to wear a German uniform with swastikas stamped on it was so revolting it nauseated him. And he hoped Captain Schultzenberger would not agree to letting him eat in the dining room. If the Germans were fussy about eating in the same room with Slavs he, a Jew, was even more fussy about eating in the same room with *them*. At least down in the kitchen he didn't have Hitler staring at him whenever he looked up from his plate. And he wasn't subjected to the "Heil Hitler" salutes whenever a high-ranking officer entered or left the hall.

And he now had another reason why he should continue eating in the kitchen. He discovered it could be a vital part of his assignment. The other day as he was finishing his lunch he had heard the cook say to his kitchen help: "I want you to peel an extra sack of potatoes this afternoon. There'll be sixty more for dinner tonight." It occurred to him that this might be a clue to something worth following up, and he was right. When he got up to the dining hall he casually remarked to the pianist, "I hear there'll be a big crowd for dinner tonight."

"Who told you that?" he asked, his face assuming a somewhat rigid expression.

"Nobody told me. I just heard Barash tell the kitchen girls to peel an extra sack of potatoes because they expect more people. That's all."

"Now that you know it, Mitek, don't mention it to a soul. This has to do with the movement of troop trains. Exactly the kind of information the bandits are looking for. Barash had to be told because he's got to know how much to cook. And I had to be told because the captain wants me to work until midnight tonight. This is voluntary, of course, but if you stay with me you'll pick yourself up a nice tip, and the captain will be very pleased. What do you say, Mitek?"

"I'll stay."

"Fine, it'll make it a little easier for me."

That afternoon when Mitek reported to Keril what he'd heard in the kitchen the latter smiled and nodded. "We already know about the train that's on the way,

Mitek. A train is too large to conceal. What we don't know is who's on it. What unit from what division. That'll be your job. Get the insignia and whatever else you can pick up. And come by right after breakfast. In this case I don't want to wait till the afternoon."

This was the first time that Keril asked him to come in the morning—a sign that he attached much importance to this particular train. And Motele felt confident about the success of his assignment. He had a tried and tested method of identifying officers' insignias. Oddly enough, it was the pianist who had led him to it. During the dinner hour on his first night at the Officers House, Herr Saldowski had pointed out to him the tables where the high-ranking officers sat and told him to walk up to them and play a selection. From that time on it had become established procedure for both the lunch and dinner hour. And while his fingers moved nimbly over the strings his eyes took in every insignia on the uniforms.

One morning Motele received word from the tailor shop to come and claim his uniform. It was ready. What he had dreaded for nearly two weeks and hoped would never happen had come to pass. Reluctantly he responded to the message, trudging, heavyhearted to the tailor shop, every step of the way an effort. They made him try it on right there to see if it fitted. It fitted perfectly, the head tailor told him and then led him to a full-length mirror to see for himself.

What he beheld in the mirror was a miniature Hitler

soldier, swarming with swastikas. He felt his body growing rigid with an almost paralyzing stiffness, and he had to labor for breath, as though some invisible hand were holding him by the throat.

"Well, how does it feel?" the head tailor asked.

Motele, his eyes painfully glued to the mirror, was silent.

"Ask him in German," one of the tailors quipped. "Now that he's got this uniform on, Ukrainian doesn't suit him anymore."

There was laughter in the shop. "I do so speak Ukrainian," Motele flung at them. He was eager to get out of there as quickly as possible. He gathered his old clothing into a bundle and left the shop.

As he hurried to his lodgings people on both sides of the street stared at him with special interest, some turning their heads for a second time. A German uniform was no novelty in Ovrutch, but a German uniform on a boy his age was. Even soldiers stopped to size him up. Was the war going that badly? They all saw through him, Motele thought. A Jew in a German uniform! Else why would they stare so hard?

His landlady gasped when he appeared in the kitchen doorway. For a moment she hadn't recoginzed him. But in the next breath she scolded him. "You frightened the life out of me, Mitek. Don't play such jokes on me."

"I'm not playing any jokes," he said, holding back his tears. "I must wear this to work. They make me do it."

Seeing the pained look on his face she said, somewhat

defensively, "You never mentioned the uniform to me. Not even once."

"That's true," he said, realizing that he hadn't.

Just then the landlady's two children burst noisily into the room. A sandy-haired boy of six and his chubby, pink-faced sister two years younger. The sight of their lodger in German uniform silenced them instantly. They stared at him with apprehensive wonderment, both fascinated and repelled by what they saw. Earlier this morning he had sat next to them at the breakfast table, one of them, and now he was transformed into one of the enemy. After a long silence the boy glanced up at his mother and said, "Mommy, he's a German."

"I am not!" Motele shouted, venting his bitterness on the boy, "I am not a German!"

The startled boy instinctively moved toward his mother and Motele, not wanting to show them his tears, strode into his room, closing the door behind him. He flung the bundle of his old clothes to the floor and himself on the bed, letting the tears flow freely. He would have liked to remain in his room forever and never again set foot into the outside world. But the battered alarm clock on his bureau reminded him that in less than an hour he would have to play at the German Officers House.

The pianist studied him and nodded approvingly. "Amazing what a uniform will do," he said. "You look like a real German now. Come with me. I want Captain Schultzenberger to see you."

The captain came out from behind his desk and made him turn around slowly until he had inspected him thoroughly. "That's—more—like—it," he said in clipped tones, as though the words were goose-stepping out of his mouth. Then he returned to his chair and, focusing on Motele's face, added, "You, Mitek, are the only non-Aryan in all our occupied territories to wear the German uniform. That's quite an honor. I hope you fully appreciate it."

"Yes, sir."

Barash, the cook, took one look at him, shook his head and chuckled. Then he wiped his face with the towel hanging from his shoulder and went back to the pots on the stove. The kitchen girls giggled behind his back throughout the meal. Not a word was spoken. This reception suited his mood.

That afternoon, before going to his appointment with Keril, he went home to his room to take off the hated uniform and put on his old clothes. It was a relief to once again walk through the streets of Ovrutch without being stared at by every pair of eyes that passed him. But Keril greeted him with reserve and silence. "Why did you take off your uniform?" he finally demanded.

"I haven't seen you in the street this morning. How do you know about the uniform?"

"You're not supposed to see me in the street even when you do see me. You know that. But you haven't answered my question. You wore it to work. Why did you take it off now?"

"Because I hate it," Motele replied. "It makes me feel like lice are crawling all over me. I'll wear it to work but that's all."

"You must wear it all the time, Mitek," Keril said firmly. "In your room you wear anything you want, but in the street you should always be seen in uniform."

"Why should I?"

"Because you're no longer a beggar. You're a musician working in the German Officers House. Supposing Captain Schultzenberger had seen you on the street in this beggar's outfit. You think he'd like it?"

Motele said nothing. He knew Keril was right.

13 Motele took to staying home a lot. If he couldn't show himself on the street without his uniform then he would shun the street. He would go out only when it was absolutely necessary. It was necessary that he go to the Officers House and that he go for his appointments with Keril. After that he went straight home where he immediately got into his own clothes and was himself again.

To the landlady's children his homecoming was a daily event. They waited for him outside the house just as they had once waited for Daddy. Now Daddy was somewhere in Germany doing slave labor, and Mitek was their big "brother" and playmate. They knew that as soon as he put down his violin case he would empty his pockets and out would come cookies, bonbons, pieces of chocolate, things he found on the officers' tables on his way out. Then he would get out of his uniform and, whether he was in the mood for it or not, play some games with them in the back yard.

At times the landlady would appear in the doorway

and call out: "Children! Children! Let Mitek go. He has to practice." When that happened he knew he would have little time for practice that afternoon. The landlady was in one of her talkative moods and he knew in advance what the subject of the conversation would be—her husband. Her opening was always the same: "Any news about your father, Mitek?"

"Not yet," he would shake his head. "The captain hasn't heard yet from any of the camps."

"At least in your case there's a German captain looking for him. But who's there to look for my husband? For two whole months not a word. Not a letter. Not a postcard. Not a sign of life. God only knows where he is now and what they did to him!" And she would burst into tears.

It was painful for him to watch an older person cry. And it would have been easier to cry with her than to tell her things he didn't know were true, or would ever come to pass. But he knew what she wanted to hear at such moments and he said it with as much conviction as he could muster. "I'm sure you'll get a letter any day now," Motele would tell her.

"That's what you said last time."

"You know there's a war on. Nothing is on time these days. Maybe the train that carried his letter got hit by a bomb and it burned."

"Yes. I know this could happen. These are the thoughts I console myself with in the long hours of the night when I don't sleep. Better it should happen to a letter than to him, I tell myself."

When he thought he'd calmed her down and could go to his room she would bring out her husband's last letter and plead with him to read it to her.

"But I have read it to you more than once," he would remind her.

"So read it this once more. But read it slowly. Maybe he's telling me something between the lines he couldn't say outright."

Once, after he'd finished reading one of her husband's letters to her, she said, "When did your mother hear from your father last?"

"A long time ago," he said, being deliberately vague.

"It must be very hard on your mother. I know how she feels. You should write to her."

"How do you know I don't?"

"You *have* written to her?"

"Yes."

"How come she hasn't replied?"

"The mail is slow these days. Maybe it got lost. Who knows?"

"I hope you hear from her soon."

"I hope so too."

The next day he repeated this conversation to Keril. "What you said was all right," Keril told him. "But now we must see that you get a letter from 'Mother.' " They composed one on the spot and the next day Keril mailed it from a nearby village. It arrived several days later when they were all having breakfast. "It's from Mother," Motele announced as he tore open the envelope. Then he read it out loud:

Dearest Mitek:

Your sister and I were very happy to hear from you at last. You were lucky to land such a well-paying job with two good meals a day. Let's hope that soon there will also be good news about your father. Thank you for the money you sent. It'll sure come in handy. Do take care of yourself, Mitek, and do write often.

Your Loving Mother

"I'm so happy for you, Mitek," the landlady said, dabbing her eyes with a corner of her apron. "Maybe you'll be lucky for me. Maybe tomorrow there'll be one for me."

"I hope so," Motele said, feeling deceitful and hypocritical. He had no qualms about lying to Captain Schultzenberger. But this good-natured Ukrainian woman was herself a victim of the German occupation. To feel better he had to remind himself of what Keril had said: "We should have thought of it sooner, Mitek. It's small details like this that can trip you up. This woman is not our enemy, but a chance remark by her to someone who is could ruin the assignment and even cost you your life. One can't be too careful in this business."

Soon afterwards he himself had an experience that proved Keril's point. He had been practicing some of the German songs he knew he would be playing at the Officers House that evening. As always, as if to clear the air of the Nazi tunes, he concluded with a few popular Ukrainian songs. And as always the landlady was in the doorway of his room, singing along and swaying her head to the melodies she recognized. But that afternoon, for the first time in all his practicing, he played one of the first songs Chanele had taught him—"*Partizaner Lied.*" As soon as he became aware of the landlady's silence and the puzzled look on her face he knew he had made a mistake.

"I don't know that one," she said, "Is it a new song?"

"It's an old Russian melody I picked up somewhere. But I don't know the words."

"I like it. I wish I knew the words."

To get off that subject he struck up a lively Ukrainian tune which he knew was one of her favorites. She sang along as he played, her face animated and pleased. When it was over she clapped and said, "Thank you, Mitek. Your playing brings a little cheer into my lonely life. These songs remind me of happier days."

He put the instrument back into the case and said, "Now I've got to get dressed." She took the hint and went back to the kitchen. He closed the door and flung himself down on the bed, berating himself for having been careless. Luckily he'd only *played* "*Partizaner Lied.*" But supposing he had also sang it, as he often did with Chanele? Some Ukrainians knew a little Yiddish, especially those who had Jewish neighbors or had dealings with Jews. Yes, he was lucky he thought, and vowed to be more careful in the future.

As if having to wear the hated uniform were not enough, Motele was compelled to do something he felt was even more revolting, play the "Horst Wessel Song," the official anthem of the Nazi Party, which contained this stanza:

> *Und wenn das Judenblut vom Messer spritzt*
> *Sodann geht's nochmal so gut . . .*
> (When Jewish blood spurts from the knife
> Then things go twice as well . . .)

When he came to that part of the song he trembled all over and was off key. The pianist winced, as though he were in pain, and gave Motele a long look of rebuke. "For heaven's sake, Mitek," he said, as soon as they'd finished the number, "keep your mind on your work. This is not just another song. It's the party anthem."

"I'm sorry, sir."

"All right," the old man relented. "Even a good player can make a mistake. But since it happened I'd feel safer if we went over it a few times right after lunch."

"Yes, sir."

As soon as the last table in the dining hall was cleared

the pianist said, "All right, Mitek, let's run through it again. Just once or twice."

They were alone now in the large hall, he, the old man, and the life-size figure of Hitler staring down at them from the wall. It was the Führer's favorite song that the old man wanted him to play to perfection. Motele turned his back on that wall, as if blotting the Führer out of his range of vision would make it easier for him to go through with the ordeal. But as he was nearing the dreaded stanza the fingers on his right hand stiffened, clutching rather than holding the bow, and he bore down so heavily on the word, *Judenblut* that what came out of the instrument was a scratchy, jarring sound, as though he had moved the bow over sandpaper and not over violin strings.

The old man stopped playing, shook his head disconsolately, then turned to Motele and, in a tone of uncontrolled anger said, "What the devil got into you, Mitek? You play complicated pieces by Brahms, Mozart, and Paderewski without a single false note and you bog down over a simple melody like the 'Horst Wessel'! And twice over the same phrase! What is it about this phrase that throws you?" He leaned forward to his sheet music and, locating the phrase, recited out loud: " '*Und wenn das Judenblut vom Messer spritzt/Sodann geht's nochmal so gut . . . .*' Do you know the meaning of these words, Mitek?"

Motele shook his head.

"I thought so," said the pianist. "Here, let me translate them for you," and he began reading in Ukrainian: " 'When Jewish blood spurts from the knife then things go twice as well. . . .' That's all there's to it, Mitek," he said, in the same casual tone as he had read the translation. "Now let's take it all over again from the beginning."

Motele felt his face growing cold and white, as though the last drop of blood had been drained from it. Right now he wished that his usual embarrassment, blushing, would come to his rescue and hide his deathly pallor. Although the instrument was well tuned he began tuning it again, bending his head low in the hope that his face would regain its natural color. He sensed the old man's impatience at the piano. He had to quit stalling and start playing. "Basha, Basha," he heard himself calling for the first time in many weeks, "can you hear me?" But it was not Basha who answered his call. It was Commander Zissman. And the reply was a single word: "*Iberleben!*" Its sound in his head was clear and loud, as though it had been struck on a bell, and its effect was magical. He felt a rush of warmth to his face and straightened up. "*Iberleben!*" he silently flung at the Führer's portrait on the wall as he tucked the violin under his chin. Fear gave way to defiance. He knew now that he would play that passage right. And he did.

"That's more like it, Mitek," the pianist told him when he'd finished. "Let's go over it once more and if you do it right this time you can go home."

Later, as he was putting the violin into the case, the old man said, "If I were you, Mitek, I'd take along the music and practice a little at home. Just to make sure."

"Yes sir," Motele readily agreed, though he knew he would not play the "Horst Wessel" again till supper time. What he did practice at home was the music he truly enjoyed, the music of Bach and Brahms and Mozart. And for his landlady's benefit, especially when she was sad, he played some Ukrainian folk songs as well.

14 Motele's daily visits to Keril had by now, his third month in Ovrutch, become a set routine. Every afternoon as he approached the red brick house on a quiet side street he would look around carefully to make sure there was no Ukrainian policeman or German soldier in sight. If he saw one he would walk past Keril's house to the end of the street, go round the corner and disappear. He applied the same caution to suspicious-looking civilians. Ten minutes later he would return to see if the coast was clear. There were times when he had to walk the streets for nearly an hour before he thought it was safe to enter the house. But such occasions were rare.

But sometimes, he would meet Keril on a prearranged street corner and from there the two would walk to some deserted spot where they could talk in privacy. The reason for these outdoor rendezvous was to avoid meeting always in the same place. As Keril once explained to him: "In underground work regularity could become a trap. Change confuses the enemy."

On this particular day the meeting was at Keril's house. As always, Motele used his walking time to go over in his mind the report he was to give him while it was still fresh in his mind. The two had worked out for themselves a kind of mental shorthand for the identification of the various German troop units. Nothing was ever written down on paper either by himself or Keril. That was why on days when the report was lengthy Keril made him repeat it over and over again until he was satisfied he had committed it all to memory.

Though Keril had not told him this in so many words, Motele surmised that his reports were being transmitted daily by shortwave radio to the Partisan High Command in Moscow. He gathered this from certain remarks Keril would make from time to time: "Mitek, I want you to know they were very pleased in Moscow with yesterday's report." Or, "You'll be happy to know, Mitek, that your report was passed on to all the partisan detachments along the line, including Uncle Misha's." How else, he reasoned, could information travel that fast if not by shortwave radio? He often wondered whether Keril himself did the transmitting or someone else. But he never dared ask. In underground work you were told only what you were supposed to know; and usually at the very last minute.

The street was clear. Motele entered the house and took double steps on the winding, wooden flight of stairs. His signal was a knock, a pause to the count of ten, and another knock. He was surprised, therefore, when the door opened on the first knock. And he was more than surprised, he was startled when instead of being met by Keril he found himself face to face with an elderly, gray-bearded man. Instinctively he drew back, thinking he had knocked on the wrong door. But the man reached for his arm, whispering in Yiddish, "*Kum arein, Motele.*" He recognized the voice sooner than the face. It was Yoshke. Inside the two embraced warmly.

"It's the first time I've embraced someone in enemy uniform," Yoshke was joking a minute later.

"I wear it only to work," Motele said, defensively. "As soon as I'm back in my room I take it off."

"I must admit, the Germans have done a good job making you look like one of them. Had I passed you on the street I wouldn't have recognized you."

"I didn't recognize you either at first."

"Credit our make-up artist, Avremel. He decided to add at least twenty years to my life. And all with a bit of white flour. I'm all right so long as it doesn't rain. And so long as it's not too windy. A makeup that depends on the weather is not very reliable. But we had no time to think of something better. I had to get in here in a hurry. Luckily I got away with it. The guard on the bridge didn't even bother to look at my papers. He probably thought an ancient like me could do no mischief."

"Where is Keril?"

"Away on a mission."

"Will you take my report?"

Yoshke shook his head. "That won't be necessary anymore."

"Does that mean I'm going back with you?" he asked, his face lighting up with the expectation of freedom.

"Not yet. You still have a job to do."

"What?"

"Uncle Misha will tell you that himself."

"Uncle Misha is here, in Ovrutch?"

"Not exactly in Ovrutch, but not very far from it. Now let me tell you what he wants you to do before you see him. He wants you to find out if there are any unused rooms in the Officers House, that is, rooms that no one goes into, and where they are located. In what part of the building."

"I think I know one such room already. It's on the lower floor right outside the kitchen."

"You *think* you know. Thinking is not enough. You've got to be sure."

"I'll find out tonight."

"You have tonight and tomorrow. Uncle Misha wants the information by tomorrow afternoon. You know where the Ovrutch bridge is, don't you?"

"Yes."

"Tomorrow you go there straight from work."

"I don't come here anymore?"

"There'll be no one here tomorrow. As I said, you go to the bridge instead."

"And wait?"

"And cross it. Chances are the guards won't even stop you. But if they should ask where you're going, you're giving a private lesson in the next village. That's why it's important that you have your fiddle with you."

"I go to the next village?"

"You'll cross the bridge and keep walking until you meet a young fellow, a boy about sixteen, holding fishing tackle in his hand. You'll walk up to him and say, 'Is there a lake around here?' And he will answer you, 'Yes. Come I'll show you where it is.' You then follow him to where he leads you. Don't ask him any questions. Not even his name. Is all this clear to you, Mitek?"

"Yes."

Yoshke put his hand on Motele's shoulder and looked long at this youthful but serious face. There was a flicker of pride in Yoshke's eyes. Motele was his find. His and Berek's. And he had come a long way from that early morning when they had stumbled over him on a field, half hidden in the tall grass, clutching a violin case. The question then had been what to do with him, and how to justify the presence of a twelve-year-old fiddler in a partisan detachment. The young fiddler, it turned out, was doing very well. Indeed, so well that upon his return to the base he would be decorated in front of the entire detachment.

But that was something Yoshke could not tell him now. That was to be his homecoming surprise. What he did tell him, as he embraced him again, was "I am very proud of you, Motele." Then he led him to the door, saying, "I must be going soon and we must not be seen leaving the house together." He held out his hand, "Good luck, Motele," he half whispered before he let him out. "Next time . . . in the forest."

As he emerged from the dim hallway into the sunlight Motele was still so overwhelmed by the experience of seeing Yoshke that he had to stop and think in which direction to go. But once he found his bearings his legs carried him, as though from habit, to his lodging while his thoughts were back in the room with Yoshke, recalling every word and gesture that had passed between them during that brief half hour.

"I am proud of you, Motele." Yoshke's words! They were as reassuring as Yoshke's arms around him. When Keril would tell him that Moscow was pleased with his reports he suspected that Keril was trying to boost his morale, to give him courage to go on because he knew how unhappy he was having to wear a German uniform and having to play for Nazi officers. He himself found it difficult to believe that faraway Moscow would take note of what he was doing in Ovrutch. After awhile his reports had fallen into a set pattern. With few exceptions the type of insignia rarely varied. Only the number of officers was different from day to day. One day it would be eighteen of the Einsatzgruppen, broken down into three colonels, five majors, four captains and the rest lieutenants. Another day it might be the same number of officers but with an entirely different breakdown in rank.

In the beginning he thought he'd never succeed in his assignment, that his mind would never retain all that his eye had registered. But once he had devised a system for himself of keeping the figures in his head until he reported them to Keril his reports became a simple and dull routine that made his horseshoeing job at the family camp seem like exciting adventure by comparison.

But it was precisely the breakdown of these figures that made his reports so important to the strategists of the Partisan High Command in Moscow. They provided valuable clues to the numerical strength of the various units the Germans were sending to the eastern front. And with this information in hand the High Command was in a better position to deploy its own forces in a way that would thwart the enemy's plans or hurt him considerably.

But all this Motele did not know at the time. How could he possibly have guessed it from Keril's occasional remark that "Moscow was pleased with your report."

The landlady's children had been waiting for him at the gate and when they saw him coming they ran toward him, their shrieks of delight scattering his thoughts.

They held him firmly by his arms and led him, their willing prisoner, into the house. As he emptied his pockets on the kitchen table they crowded around him and divided the sweets between them. He was glad the landlady was not at home. He was too restless to be cooped up in the kitchen listening to her troubles, or to practice. He changed into his old clothes and when the children begged him to play with them he was ready.

The twelve-year-old boy played as a twelve year old, with zest and abandon, while the twelve-year-old partisan was off in another world, the world of signals and disguises; of playing the "Horst Wessel Song" and thinking of *Iberleben*; of serenading a German officer while "stealing" his rank with his eyes; of being Motele and Mitek at one and the same time and being constantly on guard that one did not betray the other. Even as he was leaping over the courtyard fence, with the landlady's wildly shrieking children in hot pursuit, his thoughts were on the message Yoshke had given him, and he was trying to guess why Uncle Misha needed to know about unused rooms in the German Officers House.

The waitresses were too busy setting the tables to notice that he had come to work fifteen minutes early (to have come still earlier, he reasoned, might have looked suspicious). The pianist was not there yet. He placed his violin on the piano top and went down to the lower floor. He was right. There *was* a door close to the kitchen entrance, as he had told Yoshke. He looked about him. The corridor was empty. He turned the knob and quickly entered the room.

In the semidarkness he found the light switch on the wall and flicked it on, but there was no light. Either the fixture in the ceiling was broken, he thought, or there was no bulb. At any rate, it was safe to assume that if this room was used at all it was not used at night. There were some things scattered on the floor but he couldn't make out what they were. He opened the door and slipped out unnoticed.

The next day he again came to work a little earlier and, shortly before lunch, entered the room again. It was a damp, catch-all storage room. His quick inventory revealed a broken chair lying on its back, a heap of empty potato sacks, a pair of discarded old trousers, a rusty skillet, and an empty herring barrel, still smelling of brine. He glanced up at the ceiling. The fixture, torn from the socket, was hanging precariously from a cord. There were two windows looking out on a junk heap. One of the panes was broken and the hole stuffed with a rag. As he was about to leave, his eye caught the wide, uneven crack in the wall he was standing next to. Obviously, the room was unused.

He walked the length of the corridor, bypassing the toilet for the kitchen help, which he too was obliged to use. At the very end there were two doors facing each other. On each of them hung a wooden sign saying:

Eintrit Verboten. Upstairs, in a small corridor off the dining hall, there were the officers' mens' room and the waitresses' ladies' room and nothing else. So it came down to one unused room. He hoped it would do for what Uncle Misha had in mind.

It felt odd not to go to Keril directly from the Officers House but to walk to the Ovrutch bridge instead. The guards stared at him with curiosity but did not ask to see his papers. His uniform was his identification. About a half mile past the bridge he came upon the youth with the fishing tackle. For a moment his mind went blank and he stood there with his mouth half open and not a sound coming out of it. The youth waited, his eyes on his fishing tackle. If he had any reaction to Motele's silence his face did not betray it. "Is there a lake around here?" Motele finally remembered.

"Yes," the boy sprang to life. "Come, I'll show you where it is."

The "lake" the boy led him to, through narrow, winding paths, turned out to be a wooden shed in a thickly wooded area, about a quarter of a mile off the main road. Camouflaged with twigs and branches, the shed was invisible until you were almost upon it. The boy, who had not spoken a word throughout the walk, now motioned with his hand toward the door and before Motele could find the iron handle which served as a knob, disappeared.

He entered without knocking and found Uncle Misha and Berek seated at a table, the kind that was familiar to him by now, two weathered boards on a pair of wooden horses. Except for this makeshift table and the two wooden benches on either side of it the shed was barren.

Both men rose. Uncle Misha took his violin from him and placed it on the table. Then he put his arms around him and held him close for a long moment, just as Yoshke had done the other day. To be greeted thus by the commander, of whom he was so much in awe, made him terribly self-conscious and he blushed, something that hadn't happened to him in a long time. But by the time Berek was through embracing him his face had found its normal color.

Neither of them wore a disguise since they were a good distance away from the bridge and would not come in contact with the guards. But when they spoke they lowered their voices to a half whisper, even in this secluded spot. They sat down again and Motele took the bench opposite them. "Before we talk about your new assignment, Motele," Uncle Misha began, leaning forward to bring his voice closer to his listener, "I would like to say a word about the old one. But only a word. Because we haven't the time to sing your praises. That will come later. All I want to say right now is: We are very proud of you, Motele. All of us. You've done a splendid job. But the time has come to finish it and the sooner you do that the sooner you'll be able to throw away the accursed uniform you're wearing."

"And stop playing the 'Horst Wessel Song,'" Motele added.

"Und wenn das Judenblut vom Messer spritzt sodann geht's nochmal so gut. . . ."

Motele was startled to hear the commander recite the loathsome words. Berek too looked surprised.

"I hear it daily on our shortwave radio," Uncle Misha explained. "Josef Goebbels broadcasts from Berlin the Führer's daily message to the troops in the field. The broadcast always ends with the 'Horst Wessel Song.'"

The commander's face, animated a minute ago, was suddenly clouded with sadness. This instant change of expression in the middle of a conversation was by now familiar to Motele. He had seen it on Yoshke's face and on Luba's; on Avremel's and on Feivel's; on Chanele's and on Surele's. It was enough to mention the name of a ghetto and a look of pain would come to their faces. The memory of their families was ever present in their minds. After a thoughtful pause Uncle Misha said, as if to no one in particular, "They are very brave, these Nazis, when they are mowing down defenseless women and children and unarmed men, trapped in a ghetto. But let them come face to face with an armed Jewish partisan and these Horst Wessel heroes turn into whining cowards, begging for mercy." Looking directly at Motele now he leaned forward and said, "What have you got to tell us, Motele, about the message I sent you with Yoshke?"

"I found only one room," Motele said apologetically.

"One is all we need, provided it's the right one. Is it unused?"

"I think so."

"We must be sure."

"There's no light. The fixture is torn out of the ceiling."

"Then it's not used at night. But what about the daytime?"

"I've never seen anyone going in or coming out of there."

"Tell us about it," Berek spoke up for the first time. "What's in there? Any furniture?"

Motele enumerated everything he remembered seeing in that room. Of all of them the two things the commander and Berek seemed to attach most importance to were the barrel and the crack in the wall. Particularly the latter. They wanted to know how wide the crack was and how deep. He couldn't tell them. All he remembered was that it spanned the entire wall and that it was uneven. Their interest in the crack became even more pronounced when he told them that the room was right below the dining hall.

"The first thing I'd like you to do when you get into that room tomorrow," Berek told him, "is to measure the width and depth of the crack." He reached into his breast pocket and brought out a small folding ruler. "Here," he said, handing it to Motele, "guard it with your life. I want it back tomorrow."

They went over the other things again—the broken chair on the floor, the empty potato sacks, the broken window stuffed with a rag—they all seemed to indicate that it was an abandoned, unused room. Still, it was an assumption and not a certainty. And they had to be absolutely certain. Uncle Misha turned to Berek, and for a long moment the two looked at each other in silent deliberation. Finally Uncle Misha said, "I guess we'll have to make the straw test. Even if it means a loss of three days." Berek nodded in agreement, "It's the only way to be sure," he said.

Motele looked at them blankly. He'd never heard of the straw test.

"You know what we're talking about, Motele?" Uncle Misha said.

"The straw test. But I don't know what it is."

"Very simple. Berek will show you."

Berek rose and invited Motele to come outside. From underneath the steps Berek pulled out a straw and broke off a piece about three inches long. He then opened the door a bit, held the piece of straw against the jamb, high above the door handle, and closed the door. When he removed his hand the straw was held securely between the door and the jamb. "It's hardly visible," he said, pointing to the straw, "and nobody who doesn't know it's there would pay any attention to it. Now watch this." He opened the door and the straw fell to the ground. "You have just witnessed the straw test," Berek told him. "That's all there is to it." He picked up the piece of straw and handed it to Motele. "Now you do it."

Motele went through the routine without a hitch. When he was back in the shed Uncle Misha gave him these instructions: "Tomorrow, after you will have measured the crack in the wall, begin the straw test as Berek showed you. From that moment on you will not open the door for three days, but each time you pass it glance up to see if it is still there. If after three days it is still there in the same place it will be safe to assume that the room is not being used."

"Here," Berek said, handing him the straw, "put it in your pocket. It'll save you the job of fishing one out of your mattress."

"Do I come back here tomorrow?" Motele asked Uncle Misha.

"You'll come back here three days from now when the straw test is finished. In the meantime, instead of going to Keril you'll take a walk in the afternoons across the bridge with your fiddle. The guards must become accustomed to seeing you and your fiddle together. You don't have to walk very far but take at least an hour before you return. On the third day you'll come as far as you came today and the boy with the fishing tackle will meet you again." Uncle Misha turned to Berek, "Can you think of anything else?"

"Yes. That herring barrel. Is it big enough to hold the fiddle? I mean without the case."

"I see what you mean," Uncle Misha said after a pause. Motele didn't. Just as he didn't see the importance of a crack in the wall, which he had almost overlooked altogether. A violin in a herring barrel! An odd place for a musical instrument, to say the least. Besides, didn't Uncle Misha tell him a minute ago that he must take his fiddle with him whenever he crossed the bridge? But he knew better than to ask questions. The answers would come in due time. "Yes, I think it's big enough," he said.

"To make sure measure the length of the barrel too," Berek told him.

Uncle Misha glanced at his watch. "We must be on our way," he said to Motele, "and so must you." He embraced him again, then led him to the door. "I know you'll do well. Good luck."

When Motele emerged from the shed the boy with the fishing tackle materialized as if from nowhere and led him in silence all the way back to the main road.

15 Throughout the long walk back to town Motele could think of nothing but his odd assignment—measuring a crack in the wall, measuring a barrel, wedging a straw between a jamb and a door. What will it all add up to? he wondered. He tried guessing and after several tries thought he had actually figured it all out. Berek was the clue. It was no accident that of all the partisans in the detachment Berek alone was with the commander in the shed. Berek was the detachment's demolition expert. No one could equal him in the handling of explosives. Partisans considered it an honor to be his partner on a derailing mission. If the plan was to blow up the Officers House then Berek was the right man for the job.

That explained the need for an unused room and the interest in the crack in the wall. Berek, dressed as a German officer, would enter the Officers House at a prearranged time when he, Motele, would be on hand to lead him directly to the unused room. Once inside he would mine the cracked wall with explosives. He,

Motele, would serve as his messenger and, if necessary, smuggle in some food for him. A perfect plan for blowing up the German Officers House. Then he remembered that he also had to measure the barrel to see if it would hold his violin and his whole theory fell apart. Why would they want to put his instrument, without which he would never have gotten into the Officers House, in the first line of danger? It made no sense. And if that made no sense how could it be part of a plan that did? So he was back to guessing again. But of one thing he was certain: It was a very important assignment indeed if Uncle Misha himself came that close to Ovrutch to give him the instructions.

Uncle Misha and Berek were waiting for him at the shed when, on the afternoon of the third day, he brought the measurements and the good news of a successful straw test. Berek took the folding ruler from him and checked the measurements. "This must be a brick wall and very well constructed," he said, after a pause. "The crack was no doubt caused by the impact of a bombardment, but the wall held up pretty well. It'll have to be widened. And made a little deeper too in spots." He took out a piece of paper and made some quick calculations. "I would say we'll need about eighteen kilos," he said, turning to Uncle Misha. "All we have is ten. At the most eleven."

It was the first inkling Motele had that he'd been on

the right track in his guessing. He could hardly wait for Berek to get to the barrel measurements.

"Zissman, I know, can part with about four kilos," Uncle Misha said. "We'll see what Yoshke and Keril will bring back from the Ukrainian detachment."

"Even if they bring back two kilos we'll manage."

"You know what we're talking about, Motele, don't you?" Uncle Misha said.

"Yes. Berek will get into the unused room disguised as an officer and mine the wall."

"The boy's on the right track, Berek," Uncle Misha said, smiling. "What do you say? Want to reconsider?"

"No, thanks," Berek shook his head. "I think he's just trying to talk himself out of a job."

"You hear what he's accusing you of, Motele?" Uncle Misha said. "Are you going to let him get away with it?"

"Yes," Motele said, smiling, taking in his stride the banter the two men were indulging in at his expense.

"You see, I'm right," Berek said. "He wouldn't even defend himself."

"Well, we must get on with our business," Uncle Misha said, and the seriousness of his tone instantly changed the mood in the shed. "The fact is, Motele, you were not far from right. In the beginning we did plan to do exactly as you said—get Berek into that un-used room—which, by the way, shows that you're using your head, you're thinking like a partisan. But a parti-san must weigh all the possibilities for failure as well as success before starting out on a mission, and this led us to change our plan. Berek knows all of six German words, three of which he pronounces with a Yiddish accent. If he should find himself in a situation where he has to open his mouth it's the end of Berek and the end of the mission."

"And there's another thing," Berek added, earnestly. "The crack in the wall is a piece of luck that will save us time. But even so it'll take some work to widen and deepen it. You can't chisel away continuously until you're finished or you're bound to be heard and discovered. So it has to be done piecemeal, in short periods of time; and that could take several days."

"So, considering all these factors," Uncle Misha continued, "we think you are the ideal one for the job. You're a member of the staff so you can come and go as you please; and no one expects you to speak German. Berek will show you what you have to do. When you come here tomorrow you'll get your first lesson. What do you say, Motele, you think you'll be able to do it?"

"Yes," he said, without a moment's hesitation. This was what he had been waiting for all these months. "Basha! Basha!" he heard himself calling silently, "it is happening! I am going to avenge you. You and Pappa and Mamma and our teacher whom they hanged from a tree, and our neighbors whom they burned alive in their huts." And he thought of Chanele's and Surele's dear ones; of Yoshke's and Berek's; of Uncle Misha's and Luba's; and of Keril's brother, the partisan, who was hanged. And he thought of the pits. . . . There was not a single Jew in Uncle Misha's detachment, or in the family camp who had not lost someone to the pits! And when he thought of the pits, the heap of Jewish corpses was so staggering that he wished he could be in a thousand German Officers Houses all at the same time. Suddenly he turned to Uncle Misha and said with alarm, "The others. What about the others?"

"What others?" Uncle Misha wanted to know.

"The Ukrainians who work in the Officers House. The waitresses. The cook and the kitchen girls. The pianist. They might get . . . killed."

"Don't you know yet, Motele," Uncle Misha said calmly, "that we, partisans, mete out partisan justice only to Nazis and their collaborators. Before you put that lighted match to the fuse make sure that all these people are out of the building. There must be no innocent victims."

Something was still bothering Motele. He'd mentioned the pianist but had not told Uncle Misha that the man was a Volksdeutscher. Volksdeutsche had a reputation for being collaborators. The old man had been kind to him but he had no way of knowing what he had done in the past, or what he was doing now, after working hours. "Uncle Misha," he said hesitantly.

"Yes, Motele."

"The pianist is a Volksdeutscher. But he's an old man," he added quickly.

"Age has nothing to do with it. Motele. How young must one be to point out a Jewish hiding place to the Germans? One motion with a finger and the Jew is dead. That pianist you mentioned, how do *you* feel about him?"

"He's been kind to me and tried to help me whenever possible."

"But do you know anything about his activities outside the Officers House?"

Motele shook his head.

"In the course of your working with him did he ever say anything that would make you think he was a collaborator?"

"No."

Uncle Misha turned to Berek and the two had a silent exchange, a deliberation with their eyes only. Then he said to Motele, "In that case treat him as you would all the other help."

Motele sighed in relief. He was glad Uncle Misha gave the pianist the benefit of the doubt. He couldn't live with himself if he thought he was in some way responsible for the death of an innocent person.

"Now please take out the fiddle," Berek said.

Motele took out the instrument and placed it on the table. Berek measured it and compared the measurement with that of the barrel. "It's a large barrel," he announced. "It can easily hold two such fiddles."

Both men now gave the empty case a thorough going over, tapping the frame with their knuckles, running their fingers over the small hinges that united top with bottom, lifting it to gauge its weight, while Motele followed their motions with increasing bafflement. Finally Berek produced his pocket ruler again and measured the case for length, width, and depth. After a thoughtful pause he said, "I would say three kilos is the maximum it could hold. I wouldn't take a chance on more."

"This means five or perhaps six trips," Uncle Misha said.

"Yes," Berek nodded. "But it'll take as many days for him to learn what he has to do. So there's no time lost."

"Have we given some thought to where he'll keep all the explosives he'll bring in each day?" Uncle Misha asked.

"That's no problem, now that we know the size of the barrel," Berek said. "It's deep enough for both."

Now that all the pieces of the puzzle had at last fallen into place, Motele was horrified at the thought of his violin sitting on a heap of explosives. The violin was his most precious possession. He knew there was no reason for his alarm, that dynamite does not explode by itself, without ignition. But knowing this did not make him any less apprehensive about the safety of his instrument. His anxiety must have shown on his face, for when Berek looked up at him he said, "All that could happen to your fiddle is it'll smell of herring a little. That's still better than leaving it on a damp floor."

Berek's words were reassuring. Still, he tried to think of another hiding place for the violin. In the end he had to settle for the barrel. The ideal place was the piano top. But how could he leave his instrument there while he was coming and going with an empty case? What if the old man arrived early one day, saw the violin but the violinist *and* the case were not there? So it had to be the barrel.

"You can put your fiddle back in the case," Berek said. "And I'll see you here tomorrow at the same time."

"And I'll see you in the forest when it is all over," Uncle Misha said, taking Motele's hand into both of his and shaking it warmly.

The forest! At that moment it seemed like an eternity away.

16 He had been alone with Berek for over an hour, getting his first lesson in constructing a bomb from small blocks of explosive, and a demonstration in how to enlarge the crack in that part of the wall where the bomb was to be inserted. Both operations, Berek had told him, required infinite care and patience but the latter was particularly nerve-wracking because tapping a chisel with a hammer made a sound. He showed him a simple way to muffle the sound by wrapping a piece of cloth around the head of the chisel. But even a muffled sound could arouse the suspicion of a sensitive ear. This meant that the tapping had to be done lightly for brief periods of time only.

After distributing the bits of explosive throughout the bed of the violin case, Berek managed to find room also for the small chisel and the short-handled hammer he had brought for Motele. Then he padded everything thoroughly with rags to keep the objects from rattling around in the case.

Because there was no light in the room Motele could

work on the wall only in daytime. Berek had warned him it would be a nerve-wracking job and it was. Every time he heard footsteps in the corridor he imagined it was Schultzenberger heading straight for this room. He would stop tapping, the hammer poised over the chisel, his ears straining.

By the time he began his second go at the wall, in the afternoon, he had found the right strength of force for the hammer and the proper angle for holding the chisel. He was now tapping away at a steady rhythm and for much longer stretches of time than in the morning.

Before he left the room he picked up all the pieces of plaster that had fallen to the ground and put them into one of the empty potato sacks that lay in the corner. Then he tiptoed out of the room. As he wedged the straw back in its place between the jamb and the door he looked at it gratefully and felt like saying, "Good-bye, trusted friend."

Berek followed the progress of his work on the wall through the measurements he brought him daily. Despite the limited time and the many interruptions he was making headway. "One more good go at it," Berek told him on the fourth day, "and it will be finished."

It was! But it took yet another day—a sixth—to complete the transfer of the explosives from the shed to the Officers House, and that extra day was used to good advantage. Berek went over with Motele the entire operation. When he had finished he said, "From this moment on you're on your own. If you make a mistake there'll be no one to correct you. But if you remember what you have to do you have nothing to worry about. I should add this piece of advice though: Keep a cool head and a steady hand. If you get flustered stop until you calm down. That's how mistakes are made. Even by those who know their business."

"Did you ever get flustered?"

"In the beginning, yes," he said, sighing. "More than once I saw a trainload of Nazis and their equipment speed by over the mined tracks, as though nothing had happened. All because in the last moment my hand was not steady. It takes only a tiny mistake to make all your labor worthless. Fortunately, with trains there is always the hope that some other partisan detachment will get them. But you have only one chance. You mustn't miss it. If you feel you're getting tense and flustered, stop. You're not working against an oncoming train where you have only minutes to do your work. When you have everything done up to the point of ignition, report to Keril." He rose and extended his hand to Motele. "You're a good pupil," he said. "I know you will carry out your mission well. The next time I see you it will be in the forest."

These were Yoshke's parting words to him. And Uncle Misha's too. They reminded him of the words in a prayer Reb Pinches had taught him: "Next year in Jerusalem." To a partisan it was next time in the forest.

Motele had reached the main highway and was still a half a mile from the Ovrutch bridge. He was thinking of Berek. He had gotten attached to him during these past six days and now he missed him as he had missed Yoshke when the two were separated for the first time. Back in the days when he was Avremel's helper in the supply tent Berek was his unseen hero, always off on some daring mission or creating mechanical miracles with his magical fingers. He would lie awake nights, dreaming of the day when he would be galloping his horse, side by side with Berek's, on the way to a mission. Instead, he ended up shoeing horses in Feivel's smithy. Now he would be carrying out a mission himself and his hero, Berek, was confident that he would carry it out well. For the first time he was beginning to feel like a real partisan.

And now, after the sixth lesson from the master himself, the dream was sparked to life again. Was it too much to hope that when this mission was over and he was back in the forest Berek would choose him as his partner for a train-derailing mission?

But what about Chanele? Going on missions with Berek meant staying in Uncle Misha's detachment. He might never see her again. The thought upset him. In his long and lonely days in Ovrutch he had thought about her often. At times he even talked to her as he once had to Basha. He couldn't imagine himself not seeing Chanele again.

But why must it be either one or the other? he asked himself. The family camp too had a combat detachment. Not only to feed and protect the Jerusalem of the forest but also hit the enemy, destroy his food supplies, blow up his ammunition dumps. Even derail a troop train from time to time. He would persuade Commander Zissman to send him out on missions. What better recommendation did he need than having been taught by Berek himself. And he would repeat to the commander Berek's own words: "You are a good pupil. I have confidence in you." Now he was at peace with himself and he turned his thoughts to the task ahead.

When he reached the Ovrutch bridge he found a long line of foot and wagon passengers stretching all the way to the other end of the bridge, something he had never seen before. The line barely seemed to move. Inspection at the other end was very thorough. Passengers were searched from head to foot, and wagons were turned inside out.

"What are they looking for?" Motele asked an elderly peasant who was last in line.

"They don't tell you," the old man replied, "but I hear they're looking for eggs."

"You're kidding me," Motele told him. "They're searching people's pockets."

"The kind of eggs they're looking for, fellow, people keep in pockets. Or don't you know."

"They're not eggs to make an omlette with but they

can sure scramble up things," someone said and earned himself a laugh from the crowd.

"You mean they're looking for grenades," Motele said, embarrassed that he hadn't guessed sooner.

"At last you caught on, soldier boy," the old man was heard from again.

"I'm not a soldier boy," Motele protested. "I'm a musician. The uniform goes with the job. That's why I'm wearing it."

"Then take out your fiddle and scratch the strings a bit," the old man said. "Might as well be entertained while we wait."

"Play 'The Ant,' " someone called out, and now requests for favorites came from all sides.

Motele kept craning his head toward the bridge, ignoring their requests.

"Betcha he doesn't even *have* a fiddle," the old man drawled, as he rolled a cigarette for himself in a piece of ordinary newspaper. "It's a caseful of eggs he got there. That's why he don't play."

There was laughter all around him and Motele smiled self-consciously, as he felt himself growing pale.

"C'mon, fellow," someone challenged him, "show the man you got a real fiddle in there."

"I've got no time for horsing around," Motele said. "I'll be late for work." He left the line and walked up to one of the guards, a Ukrainian he remembered having seen earlier that afternoon. "I've got to get off the bridge," he told him, "or I'll be late for work. I've got to be at the German Officers House in less than an hour."

"*Ausweis*," the German guard said to Motele after the Ukrainian had translated his request.

Motele handed him the pass Captain Schultzenberger had given him when he was hired, stating that the bearer is an employee of the German Officers House and is allowed on the streets of Ovrutch during curfew hours. "Show this to the guards at the other end and they'll let you off," the German told him and waved him on his way.

People stepped aside to let him pass as soon as they saw his uniform, and the German guard waved him off the bridge after a quick glance at Captain Schultzenberger's pass. About two blocks away from the bridge he looked at his watch and became concerned about making it on time walking. He didn't think he would have the extra time needed to empty the explosive into the barrel and put his violin back into the case. If he could hitch a ride on some wagon it would help. But he was in better luck than that, he thought, when he saw a taxi coming off the bridge. It was full. Even the seat next to the driver was occupied. But he flagged it down anyway. Seeing the uniform the driver stopped and stuck his head out of the window, "Sorry," he pleaded, "I'm all filled up."

"I've got to get the German Officers House in a

hurry," Motele said firmly. "I don't care if I sit on the floor."

The driver turned to his passengers in the back. "I'm afraid we'll have to squeeze him in," he told them.

No one dared complain. Reluctantly they shifted in their seats to make room for the boy in uniform. The driver got out of the cab.

"Your fiddle will have to go in the trunk," he said, reaching for the case.

"I'll hold it on my lap," Motele said, tightening his grip on the case.

"What's wrong with putting it in the trunk?"

"It'll shake there. It's not good for the instrument."

"Not the way I'll put it in. Come on, I'll show you."

Motele did not budge. "I'll keep it on my lap," he insisted.

"You're a stubborn little fellow. You'll make everybody uncomfortable. And over nothing. All right, get in."

They rode in silence for several minutes. Seeing how well-dressed and well-fed the other passengers were, Motele felt uneasy in their midst. Taxi passengers in occupied Ovrutch were for the most part either black marketeers, who could afford the exorbitant fare, or German officers, who could take possession of any vehicle at will even if it meant ousting other passengers.

"I'll have to let you off in front of the main gate," the

driver called out over his shoulder, "they don't allow civilian vehicles inside the compound."

"The main gate will be good enough."

"Did they make you open your case?" the man next to Motele asked.

"No. They weren't looking for violins."

"What *were* they looking for?" another passenger asked.

"They were looking for eggs," Motele said, with a knowing air.

"Eggs in my breast pocket?" the man chuckled.

"Not chicken eggs. Hand-grenade eggs."

"It's those partisan bandits they're looking for," the driver said. "They're the ones who walk around with eggs on them."

"I hear some are Jews," one of the passengers said.

"They're all Jews," the driver spoke up again, and now they seemed to be talking all at once:

"I thought they've all been wiped out in the ghettos."

"Those in the forest haven't."

"The Germans will get rid of'm all, mark my word."

"*Iberleben!*" was Motele's silent retort.

"I read in the *Ovrutch Gazette* they've been cleaned out of the Klynov forest."

"On paper they've been cleaned out. They're still in control of Klynov."

"Then there must be hundreds of them still in the forest."

"What do *you* say, soldier boy? You haven't said a word."

"I'm not a soldier boy. I'm a musician."

"But you're working for the Germans and you're around Germans all the time. You think there are still that many of them in the forest?"

"From what I hear," Motele said, "there are still several thousand."

"Jesus and Mary!" the man next to him cried out.

For the rest of the way they rode in silence.

It was not until he was inside the gate and began the long winding walk to the Officers House that he realized how perilously close he had been to catastrophe on the Ovrutch bridge. The sheer luck by which he eluded the search and didn't let the driver take the heavy case now filled him with a sense of foreboding, bordering on anxiety. Why this thorough inspection, today of all days? Had the Germans gotten wind that something was in the air, that something was about to happen? What if the catastrophe he had avoided on the bridge had already struck in the unused room and he was right now walking into a trap? The straw would tell. But what if he came to the door and found the straw on the ground, should he enter or disappear as quickly as possible? These thoughts set off a violent pounding in his chest and an impulse to turn around and run. But his legs carried him forward, as though propelled by a determi-

nation of their own. He had frightened himself to death. The straw was there just where he had wedged it in the day before!

The next morning he was back at the wall, inserting the explosive in the widened crack. When he'd finished he checked to make sure that the capsule, detonator, and Bickford wick were in the right place. All that was left for him to do was to ignite the wick. He was ready to see Keril for further instructions.

Keril, who was never effusive in his greetings, now greeted him with the same display of emotion as Yoshke had twelve days ago in this same room. He embraced him and held him close to himself. "I am so happy to see you, Mitek," he said, rocking him back and forth before releasing him from his embrace. "Never in all my days in the underground was I so worried as I was that afternoon. You were very lucky. Even Volksdeutsche are made to turn their pockets inside out on these searches. By the way, what made you take a taxi, something you've not done on previous days?"

"Because I was afraid I'd be late. How do you know I took a taxi? Were you there?"

"Not I. Someone else was. Someone you don't know."

"Then how did he know it was me?"

"How many boys are there in Ovrutch who wear a German uniform and carry a violin case?"

"That's right," Motele said, somewhat embarrassed

that he'd asked the question. "But how did he know there was going to be a search? When I crossed the bridge on the way to Berek everything was quiet."

"Some of our people work in German offices. Sometimes we get warnings well enough in advance to do something about it. But these searches are surprise actions. We found out about this one too late to stop you from going across, so the best we could do was post one of our men to see if you made it back safely. And thank God you did," he added after a pause. "I'd hate to think what would happen if you didn't."

"Someone on the bridge said they were looking for eggs. You know, hand grenades. The taxi driver said they were looking for partisan bandits."

"They've never yet caught a partisan on that bridge," Keril said. "But after each search you can read in the *Ovrutch Gazette* that they caught several bandits and executed them. I take it you have something to tell me, Mitek."

"It's finished."

"Then you're all set."

"Yes. Will I do it tonight?"

Keril shook his head. "Uncle Misha is the one to decide when it's to be done, and he doesn't even know yet that you're ready. Besides, if you did it tonight how would you get out of Ovrutch?"

"I'll cross the bridge and keep on walking until I meet that fellow who doesn't talk and he'll take me to the

shed. From there someone will take me to Klynov. Maybe Berek."

Keril smiled, nodding. "You have it all figured out nicely, except that it's all wrong. After nine o'clock the bridge is closed to all traffic except the military."

"I have a pass that permits me to be on the streets during curfew."

"A bridge is not a street, Mitek. And the guards who saw you in the daytime may not be on duty at night. What if they want to know where you're going at that hour? Are you giving private lesssons at midnight?"

"So I'll cross the bridge in the morning."

"If you haven't left Ovrutch right away, by the time morning comes around you'll be in the hands of the Gestapo. The guards at the gate will know that you were the last of the employees to leave the Officers House, so you'll be the first person the Gestapo will be looking for."

Motele sat in silence, thinking how much he still had to learn about caution in the underground.

"So you see," Keril continued, "you must get out of Ovrutch that very night, and you can't use the bridge."

"Is there another way than the bridge?"

"Yes. But it's long and roundabout and takes time to prepare. That's one reason why it can't be done to-night. The other reason, as I have said, is that Uncle Misha has to decide the time." He rose and said, "Let's go, Mitek." Without asking where, Motele followed him out.

It was not until they had crossed the main square and reached the quiet side streets that Motele got an inkling as to the purpose of their walk. Keril looked about him and when he saw no one within earshot he half whispered to Motele, "Try to remember where you are, Mitek. These are the streets you'll take."

Motele noticed that they were in a heavily bombed section with hardly a whole building in sight. Not once had they come upon a German soldier or a Ukrainian policeman. Indeed, there were hardly any people at all on these streets. Both on his walks with Keril and his own wanderings through town he had never been to this part of Ovrutch.

After about twenty minutes of walking they came to a dead end, a desolate strip of land that led to the bank of a quiet, lazy-flowing river, narrow in some parts and wider in others. On the other side of the river, and for about a mile beyond it, there was a field that stretched to the edge of a forest. He followed Keril along the bank till they came to a narrow part of the river and sat down. They were completely alone here and Keril could use his natural voice. "This is the spot you want to get to," he told him. "Here you cross over to the other side."

"I'm a good swimmer," Motele said, "but what about the violin?"

"You don't have to swim. In this spot the water is up to your chest. Once you're on the other side there'll be a wagon waiting for you. Look around to make sure you remember the place." After a pause Keril turned to

Motele. "Mitek, if you had to pick the night, what night would you pick?"

"Saturday night," Motele replied at once.

"Why Saturday night?"

"Because it's the busiest and most crowded night in the Officers House. Many of the officers stationed in Ovrutch are off duty that night and they all come to the *Offizieren Haus*."

"Then that's the night it'll probably be."

"This Saturday?"

"If they can make it on time to meet you. But you be ready just in case they can."

"I *am* ready."

"I mean about knowing your way to this place. It'll be night and all you'll have is the moon. If you get lost you're lost for good. Between now and Saturday afternoon you've got to get so familiar with this walk that your legs will take you here on their own. That's what I mean by ready."

On their walk back Motele led the way with Keril close behind him, correcting him whenever he was about to make a wrong turn. When they reached the square Keril whispered, "See you Saturday afternoon," and they each went their separate ways.

Saturday morning, soon after breakfast, Motele took his fourth and last practice walk to the river bank. And if one counted the walks back it would be the eighth. By then his legs did indeed take him there on their own.

All along the way he had picked signs for himself large enough to be visible even on a dark night—a mangled heap of debris, a brick chimney jutting out of a bombed structure like a giant finger pointing to the sky, a lone house, untouched by the war—these and other signs he had committted to memory were to guide him unerringly to his destination. He was ready now and he hoped that when he saw Keril this afternoon the word from Uncle Misha would be yes for tonight. Waiting for that word became as tense and nerve-wracking an experience as was the tapping on the wall in those stolen moments of mornings and afternoons.

As he was approaching the isolated area his eye caught a figure wading in the river. He stopped. It was the first time in his practice walks that he had come upon another human being in this desolate spot. He wondered whether he should go on or turn around and disappear. But before he could make up his mind what to do the figure was waving to him. Now he had no choice but to continue. To flee would arouse suspicion. He moved cautiously, his eyes fixed on the figure. The face, which a while ago was still blurred by distance soon became clearly discernible. It was Keril! By the time Motele reached the river Keril had stepped out of the water and stood there on the bank waiting for him. He was barefoot, his trousers rolled high above his knees. "This is the spot," Keril said, turning around to face the water. "This is where you'll cross. It's the shallowest part of the river."

"When will I cross it?"

"Tonight. That's why I'm here. To find the right spot. And I found it. Stay here a minute. Don't move." He strode off in his bare feet to a barren tree, a distance of about fifty yards, and broke off a branch. He then stuck the branch deep into the soft earth by the bank. "This will mark the spot," he told Motele. "You can't miss it." He sat down on the ground and rubbed his feet dry, first with his bare hands and then with his handkerchief before he pulled his socks and boots on again. Then he stood up and put his hand on Motele's shoulder. "Mitek," he said, looking long into Motele's face, "my job is finished. You'll finish yours tonight."

"Will I see you this afternoon?"

"There's no need to. You already know it's tonight. You know your way to the river and where to cross. And I'd rather we didn't leave this place together. Not today." He took Motele's hand. "I'll miss you, Mitek."

"I'll miss you too."

"Let's make a pact," he said, clasping Motele's hand with both of his, "if we survive this war we'll meet again and celebrate. You come to Ovrutch or I'll come to your home. Makes no difference."

"I'll come to Ovrutch." Right now he had two homes, and they were both in the forest. In one he had Yoshke and in the other he had Chanele. But after the war—what Jew could speak of a home after the war?

"It's a deal," Keril said, shaking Motele's hand vigorously. "And good luck tonight." Then he turned and walked away.

Motele stood there, following Keril with his eyes, watching his only contact with the forest disappear. Now he was alone in Ovrutch. Completely alone. He sat down next to the branch Keril had pushed into the ground and looked at it appreciatively. Like the straw wedged to the doorjamb it too was now the trusted keeper of a secret.

He was aware of the quiet around him. Even the water flowed soundlessly. Beyond it was the field, and beyond that the forest, clearly visible in the morning brightness. It was from there his liberators would come. In a wagon, Keril had told him. How could a wagon come through a forest? Probably on a road one couldn't see from here with the naked eye. Else why would Keril have said a wagon? He wondered if Yoshke would be on that wagon. Or Berek. Or maybe Uncle Misha himself. He glanced at his watch. In less than fourteen hours he should be back here, crossing the water and running toward the wagon. His job done and free at last!

The thought should have made him happy. Then why did he feel so sad, so utterly, so terribly alone? Why could he not hold back the tears? Maybe it was because of this place. It reminded him so much of Stare-Mloda. A few minutes walk from his house and he and Basha were on a river bank, or in a field, or in a forest, singing duets, or she was singing and he accompanying her on the violin. Or maybe they were just walking and talking for hours about the same friends, the same teachers, and their dreams of someday leaving this little village and going out into the big world, maybe even all the way to America where they had some relatives, and where he would become a famous concert violinist and she a famous singer.

Now he didn't even know where Basha and his parents were buried. Stare-Mloda had no Jewish cemetery, and who would have bothered to take them to town, where village Jews were brought for burial? The last time he saw them they were all lying on the floor, and that is how he would always remember them.

He reached for the violin case, as if to go, but instead snapped it open, took out the instrument, and began to play *"Partizaner Lied,"* the song Chanele had taught him, the song he'd played nightly at the family camp campfires. He could hear the young people sing and the forest reverberate with their voices:

> A girl, a jacket, a beret
> A pistol firmly in her hand
> A girl with a velvet face
> Struck the enemy caravan
>
> At dawn she slipped out of the forest
> A garland of snow in her hair
> The victory was small but oh, how sweet!
> A victory for the freedom day.

He put his violin back into the case, rose to his feet,

took a last look at the branch to fix it in his mind, and then walked back to town.

Motele arrived at the Officers House at half past five and before entering the building he took a quick glance at his freshly pressed uniform and polished boots to make sure that everything was in order. A kind of self-inspection before the weekly ritual of being inspected by the old man.

The dining hall bore all the signs of the usual Saturday night event—the scrubbed floor, the swastikas draped around the Führer's portrait, the waitresses bustling about in freshly starched uniforms. Hanging from the ceiling was a large sign saying: WILKOMMEN SS— SIEG HEIL! From this he gathered that the highest ranking officer to have arrived in Ovrutch today was from the SS.

As soon as the pianist, dressed in a tuxedo, had looked him over and nodded approval, Motele started for the stairway leading to the kitchen. Not that he was hungry. If anything he was too nervous for food right now. What he wanted most was a last, reassuring look at the straw.

"Just a minute, Mitek," the old man called after him. "Before you go down for your supper come with me. The captain wants to see you."

For an instant Motele felt as though his heart had stopped beating. For the first time since he had come to Ovrutch he was seized by fear and he tried desper-

ately not to show it. "You know what it's about?" he
asked.

"How should I know. Come down and you'll find out."

He followed closely behind the pianist, clenching his
fists to keep his hands from trembling. "They can tor-
ture me to death," he said to himself, "and I will not
betray Keril. I will not betray anybody." Miraculously,
his firm resolve swept away his fear. He was resigned
to the worst.

The captain, freshly shaved, the buttons on his uniform polished to a high luster, leaned far back in his
chair, his head almost touching Hitler's portrait on the
wall behind him. "Mitek," he said, letting the chair
spring back to his desk, "I'm afraid the news I have
for you is not very good."

By now Motele knew enough German to have caught
the drift of what the captain had said even before the
old man translated it into Ukrainian. "This came this
afternoon," the captain said, holding up a sheet of paper. "Let me read it to you: 'I regret to inform you that
there is no prisoner by the name of Ivan Dubinov in
any of the camps under my command. Nor is there a
record of the above-named prisoner to show that he had
ever been in any of the camps in the Zhitomir area.'
You see, Mitek," the captain said, leaning back again,
"somebody must have given you the wrong information.
Your father is in some other place. And I think it would
be foolish on your part to wander all over the Ukraine

to look for him. If he's alive he'll show up sooner or later. In the meantime you have good food and you're wearing a German uniform. What more can one ask in wartime?"

"Yes, sir."

"Tonight, Mitek, you'll play for a German general. A great honor. Play well."

"Yes, sir."

When the general made his entrance with Captain Schultzenberger at his side, the assembled officers sprang to their feet and for several minutes made the walls shake with their "Sieg Heils." Then they burst into song with *"Deutschland Uber Alles"* followed by the "Horst Wessel Lied." As always, when they came to the phrase: "When Jewish blood spurts from the knife then things go twice as well," Motele flung back at them silently, *"Iberleben! Iberleben!"*

Officers House dinners were long and elaborate affairs and the menu came from all parts of occupied Europe—meat and vegetables from the Ukraine, fish and caviar from Russia, vodka from Russia and Poland, wines and liqueurs from France, cheese from Holland and Denmark, fruit from Czechoslovakia, pastry from Austria. Chocolate was the exception. It came from neutral Sweden and Switzerland. On Saturday nights the kitchen stayed open till eleven, but drinking went on till the wee hours of the morning.

A little after twelve the old man relinquished the piano to one of the officers and went home. Soon other officers, their drinks in hand, drifted over and the nightly session of bawdy ballads and sentimental soldier songs was in progress.

Motele kept an eye on the door, counting the waitresses as they were leaving for home. When the last one had left he ran down to check on the kitchen. Barash and his help were still cleaning up. He would wait until they too were gone, no matter how long it took. There must be no innocent victims. Twice more he had to go down before he saw the lock on the kitchen door. Then he made one final check in the help's toilet and went upstairs for his violin. He slipped out of the dining hall without being noticed by anyone.

From sheer habit he glanced up at the straw before putting his hand on the knob. On the first match he made it to the wall. Then he struck another match and put it to the wick.

He hurried through the long corridor to the back door and kept up this rapid pace all the way to the main gate. "*Gute nacht*," he said to the guards and disappeared into the night.

Could ten minutes be that long? He thought it would never happen when the first blast came and shook the ground beneath him. A flash of light streaked the sky like lightning. Then another and another. He ran without being aware that he was touching ground. He was flying through the streets. He shot a backward glance and saw a roaring Gehenna behind him. He heard sirens whining in the distance but was not afraid. Their sound seemed to lend strength to his legs and breath to his lungs. Another street . . . another blast . . . another alley . . . another blast. . . . "Basha! Basha! Can you hear it?"

Breathing hard, he ran all the way to the dead-end area. The branch Keril had stuck into the ground in the morning gave him his bearings. He stepped into the river. The sudden rush of cold water against his warm body wrenched a sigh from his throat. He held his violin case aloft as he waded laboriously ashore. Then he paused, his eyes searching the field on a moonlit night. He spotted the wagon and ran toward it with renewed strength. Yoshke's strong hands reached out to him and pulled him into the wagon. As they rode off Motele turned for a last look at Ovrutch. The burning Officers House lighted up the sky like a giant torch. "That's some candle you lit there," Yoshke said, pulling Motele close to him.

"A *yartzeit* candle for our dead," one of the partisans added.